FV_

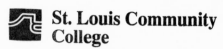
St. Louis Community College

Forest Park
Florissant Valley
Meramec

Instructional Resources
St. Louis, Missouri

GAYLORD S

MEN!

I MAINTAIN THAT WHEN MEN ARE PERFECT,
WOMEN WILL FOLLOW THEIR EXAMPLE.

CHRISTINE DE PIZAN

EDITED BY BETTY JANE WYLIE

MEN!

QUOTATIONS
ABOUT MEN,
BY WOMEN

KEY PORTER·BOOKS

Canadian Cataloguing in Publication Data

Main entry under title:

Men! : quotations about men, by women

ISBN 1-55013-516-3

1. Men - Quotations. 2. Quotations, English.
I. Wylie, Betty Jane, 1931-   .

PN6084.M4M46 1993   305.31   C93-094230-2

Key Porter Books Limited
70 The Esplanade
Toronto, Ontario
Canada M5E 1R2

Illustrations: Kathryn Adams
Design: Annabelle Stanley

Distributed in the United States of America
by National Book Network, Inc.

Printed and bound in Canada
93 94 95 96 97 6 5 4 3 2 1

To all my male friends, in the hope that they still are

CONTENTS

ACKNOWLEDGEMENTS

Grateful acknowledgement is made to those who have given permission for the use of previously copyrighted material in this book. Every possible care has been taken to acknowledge copyright information correctly. The editor and publisher would welcome information that will enable them to rectify any errors or omissions in succeeding printings. A complete list of sources can be found at the end of the book.

The editor would also like to thank the stalwart women at the MacTier Post Office, Pamela and Joyce and Barb, who look after her even when faced with a blizzard of mail such as this book caused.

The publisher gratefully acknowledges the assistance of the Canada Council and the Government of Ontario.

·INTRODUCTION·

❤

"Anything you say may be used against you," goes the warning when a person is arrested. People convict or absolve themselves with their own words. If we gather enough evidence from what a number of people have said over the years we can begin to get an idea of what they're all about, not only the people themselves but also their subjects.

Over their lives—over all our lives—women have reacted to men, to men's behavior and actions and their treatment of those closest to them, and to their relationships with each other and with their wives, mothers and children. For the most part the womenfolk have been silent, or been silenced. For centuries no one (read: man) paid attention to what a woman had to say—or write.

Women were kept illiterate, still are (80 percent of the world's illiterate today are women), and when they did learn to read and write, what they wrote was suppressed in a number of different, effective ways. Women's writing has been ignored: "Hide it in your dresser drawer, don't let it out of the house"; trivialized: "It's about children or family or feelings, not important"; doubted: "It must have been written by a man, or with a man's help"; erased: "Poor dear, she tried, let it go out of print"; denigrated: "This is a woman's book"; discredited: "Real women couldn't possibly know/write about such things"; or pilloried: "How dare she write about such things!" It's a wonder that any women's writing survived at all.

Early women writers whose work did survive were frequently anonymous. (It was Virginia Woolf's theory that "Anon" was often a woman.) Little wonder that such a small percentage of those who made their way into the great collections of quotations were women, even a smaller number than the current average 15 percent who are included in literary anthologies.

Women are making up for lost time and space now; I know of more than half a dozen books of quotations by women that have been published within the last two years, usually general in focus and contemporary in emphasis. These sayings, recovered from old and new books as well as from current newspapers and interviews, comprise a distillation of the thoughts of women as they deal with their lives and times. In the general collections, layered in amongst the cogent aphorisms and sharp insights, are comments about men, neither hidden nor stressed. This collection serves to bring some of them together and out in the open.

Past as well as present expression is examined to show what women of all ages and over the ages really think of men, and how consistently they have been thinking it. For example, in the 15th century Anon complained about her lover's infidelity:

He said to me he would be true,
And change me for none other new;
Now I sykke and am pale of hue,
For he is far.

Has anything changed?
Some things change a lot; others don't change enough. Time-

eroded complaints about men's behavior are as bitter and ignored today as at the time they were lodged. Others are new, though not very, reflecting simple changes in lifestyle rather than any significant changes in male behavior. Literate women used to have servants to do some of the dirty work; now they hope that their husbands will at least take out the garbage.

Ideas are repeated, as in all collections, and the repetition is fun. The same themes and expressions do keep popping up, so similarly phrased that one cannot help but wonder if the latter thinker had access to the first one's thoughts. Canadian suffragist Nellie McClung attributed to a friend this comment about men's egos: "Men are afraid of women, jealous of them, and unfair to them. They want women to be looking-glasses, albeit false ones that make them look bigger than they are." This was said in Alberta some time in the early 1920s.

"Women have served all these centuries as looking-glasses," wrote British novelist Virginia Woolf, "possessing the magic and delicious power of reflecting the figure of man at twice its natural size." The line is from *A Room of One's Own*, first published in 1929. I doubt that Virginia had read Nellie McClung.

"A man has only one escape from his old self: to see a different self—in the mirror of some woman's eyes," wrote American playwright Clare Boothe Luce in 1937. Contemporary feminist Kate Millett has corroborated the idea: "To each masquerading male the female is a mirror in which he beholds himself." Great minds think alike and women often agree—when it comes to men.

Women can be funny, when they are not rueful or angry. The humor comes through in self-mockery as much as in anything directly aimed at men. Is that preservation of self or of the male ego?

Of course, everyone in the past was more reticent about bodily functions and parts. Some of the funniest, most explicit lines have been uttered in this century, frequently about the penis, the male thing that women are supposed to envy. The comments don't come across as penis envy. (As one little girl is reported by her mother to have said, in serious awe after she had seen her first penis, "Isn't it lucky it isn't on his face?") American feminist Dorothy Dinnerstein refers to it as a water toy; pop star Yoko Ono says if she were a man and had that "delicate long thing hanging outside their bodies which goes up and down by its own will" she would never stop laughing at herself. But as many women have pointed out, men fear women's laughter. Therefore women have been careful not to let them hear it.

As for the anger, men haven't listened to it, don't listen. Even now, a woman's rage is dangerous—for a woman—because a man might get mad back. Fear of retaliation, both mental and physical, has kept women and women's tongues, firmly in place. "Best way over a wall is around it," and "Catch more flies with honey than with vinegar." Are these sayings phrased by women as advice to each other in order to avoid confrontation, or were they handed to them by men as the way to get along? Put up or shut up, be polite and be quiet: these have been the limited alternatives over the years. As Florida Scott-Maxwell said, the only safe place for a woman to put her foot down is in her diary. Now women's words, taken in aggregate, tell us what we knew we knew but didn't want to acknowledge, and tell men what we know about them and about our relationships with them. Is anyone listening yet?

I took a look at all the aphorisms, maxims, sayings and proverbs about men and selected basket clauses in which to gather related ideas. Thus, "Boys will be boys" catches not only the boy before he becomes a man but also the boy in the man, and the wondrous male ego, always present from birth to death.

"They're only after one thing." Men aren't the only creatures who feel desire and passion. Some men today are experiencing what it's like to be a sex object, as women have been over the centuries. How do the objects perceive being beheld? For the most part with grace, though bubbles of resentment break that deceptively smooth surface. The best way is Mae West's, with humor: "Is that a gun in your pocket, or are you just glad to see me?"

"Friendship is impossible between a man and a woman." How many times have we heard that? Yet the best of us, both women and men, work at a relationship that encompasses friendship, trust and, of course, love. *Relationship* is a twentieth-century word, but women have expressed their opinions of male-female relationships for centuries. Some still keep hoping for a prince to come; others have a more realistic view. Few have given up altogether, despite the odds.

"A man's home is his castle," and often his nursery, according to Clare Boothe Luce. The private view of men undressed, as it were—the kid's-eye view, the wife's perspective—brings home a few truths stated with unblinking clarity but also with staunch loyalty. Women take full responsibility for their families and their men. United they stand, divided they fall, and no one's going to fall if they can help it. Are we talking about patriarchy or family? In other centuries they were indivisible; now we're not so sure. The way a man treats his family often reflects his attitudes to women outside the home. By this time we all know that the personal is political. The patriarchal must be nonpartisan, if it knows what's good for it.

"Man works from sun to sun," and we all know the corollary to that one: "woman's work is never done." Women have watched, like good, admiring spectators, over the centuries while the knight goes out to kill his dragon. Men's money, status, achievement—what do they all mean to women, and where do women fit into this man's world? Even as women in the 20th century are striving for equal pay, their work is still as unequal as it is inequitably recompensed. I quote the statement made to the United Nations Women's Conference in 1980 acknowledging that women do two-thirds of the world's work.

Ah, but we speak in alien tongues. "They just don't speak the same language." And when *they* don't understand, they shake their heads and say, "Isn't that just like a woman?" But they don't mean it as a question. Even if it were they wouldn't hear the answer. Women know: men interrupt (any number of women comment on this sad fact); they don't understand; they misinterpret; they don't listen. That's just in the spoken word. As for the written one, women are finally realizing that when men write "men" they mean men. When they write about humanity, they mean men; when they write about the human condition, they mean the condition of being male. As for women—flawed men?—their acknowledgement of this blinkered half-world view has been rueful, more baffled than bitter. Five centuries ago the Italian writer Christine de Pizan wondered "how it happened that so many different men—and learned men among them—have been and are so inclined to express both in speaking and in their treatises and writings so many wicked insults about women and their behavior."

"Boys don't cry." Aye, there's the rub. They've all been brought up to be little soldiers and not to have feelings. On the other hand, beware the man who has too many feelings; he won't listen to yours. Women over the centuries have been most aware of and most protective of the vulnerable side of the male animal. Men have a lot of fears to deal with, not the least of them their fear of women. The closer we get, the more threatened they feel.

"It's a man's world," and don't you forget it. American psychiatrist Jean Baker Miller has commented on the fact that it is very difficult for the dominants to have a personal relationship with their inferiors. In order to preserve their right to rule, men must keep their control and maintain power. That means that women must be controlled and held powerless. A female view of men's dominance reveals the resentment that has been simmering in women over the centuries.

"What's sauce for the goose is sauce for the gander." The gander doesn't like to think so, however. Women's comments on the double standards that still prevail in almost every activity we undertake begin to take on an edge now. Even as women strive for political and economic equality, split-level thinking dies hard. As Jacqueline Kennedy Onassis says, "When Harvard men say they have graduated from Radcliffe, then we've made it." Don't hold your breath.

"A man is as old as he feels," goes the saying, and we know the second half of that one, too: "a woman is as old as she looks." It's a continuation of that inexorable double standard women have had to live with over the years, not without rueful comment at one's lost youth and some bitterness about what men can get away with. Susan Sontag, in her landmark essay on the double standard of aging, which appeared in *Psychology Today* in the early 1970s, recognized then the unfairness of this attitude that we still have not come to terms with. Nothing has changed, in spite of the feminist upheaval; it still falls short of revolution. As Victoria Billings says, "By fifty, a man may be at the peak of his career—with power and status. A woman is washed up."

Well, well, can't live with 'em, can't live without 'em. Can't help lovin' them. And we do—love them and make homes for them and rear their children and bolster their egos and take care of them. Even the anti-feminist Camille Paglia agrees with other women on the daily demands of looking after a man. "All men want," Paglia writes, "is approval and maintenance, day after day after day." Phyllis Schlafly, avowed enemy of the Equal Rights Amendment in the United States, sounds like any other woman when she comments on men's needs: "Whereas a woman's chief emotional need is active (i.e., to love), a man's prime emotional need is passive (i.e., to be appreciated or admired)." What can you do? Read them and weep.

The quotations game is Trivial Pursuit for the literati, not what's my line but whose line is it? Anyone can play. All you have to do is recognize a line and identify who said it. It's simple if you pay attention to what is being said, and what or whom it's being said about. But it's more than a game. Content is important. Attention must be paid.

A good line is more than the sum of its parts. It is a distillation of thought, the essence of a particular time in history, both private and public, and of the nature of the speaker or writer responding to the events in her life. In this focused selection, each quotation expresses an individual woman's life, and the man/men in it.

Thus the Japanese poet Sei Shonagon, in the 9th century, had something to say about the unfairness of a lover: "How shameful when a man seduces some helpless Court lady and, having made her pregnant, abandons her without caring in the slightest about her future!" Firmly fixed in her own time, she speaks for every betrayed woman through the ages.

On the other hand, 20th-century Canadian artist Emily Carr recognizes a universal truth in her personal lament connected with her own career: "Men painters," she writes, "mostly despise women painters."

And in between we have Jane Anger, who in 1589 expressed

her anger: "Fie on the falsehood of men, whose minds go oft a madding, and whose tongues can not so soon be wagging, but straight they fall a railing."

Past and present, public and private, an effective quotation gives us the essence of a period in history and the personality of a woman. In this collection, it gives us a woman's-eye view of men.

CAUTIONS

"WHO GOES THERE—FRIEND OR ENEMY?"

♥

If you have the bump of mirthfulness developed,
don't marry a tombstone.
FANNY FERN

Keep your eye on the man who refers to women as
the "fair sex"—he is a dealer in dope!
NELLIE MCCLUNG

Don't accept rides from strange men,
and remember that all men are strange as hell.
ROBIN MORGAN

Lady, lady should you meet
One whose ways are all discreet,
One who murmurs that his wife
Is the lodestar of his life,
One who keeps assuring you
That he never was untrue,
Never loved another one...
Lady, lady, better run!
DOROTHY PARKER

Beware of a man with manners.
EUDORA WELTY

I am very suspicious of men who want to teach me chess—
or anything else for that matter.
JOAN WYNDHAM

• B O Y S   W I L L •
B E   B O Y S

"THE ONLY DIFFERENCE BETWEEN MEN AND BOYS
IS THE PRICE OF THEIR TOYS."

❤

Man is not only an animal with a body and a being
with a brain but also a social creature who is so ineluctably
interconnected with his social group that he is hardly
comprehensible outside it....
➧ *FREDA ADLER*

Father asked us what was God's noblest work.
Anna said *men* but I said *babies*. Men are often bad;
babies never are.
➧ *LOUISA MAY ALCOTT*

Boys are always jolly,—even princes.
➧ *LOUISA MAY ALCOTT*

Yo' ain't the man yo' mamma was.
➧ *ANONYMOUS*
GRAFFITO FROM A WALL IN CHICAGO, 1971

Boys pride themselves on their drab clothing, their droopy socks,
their smeared and inky skin: dirt, for them, is
almost as good as wounds. They work at acting like boys.
They call each other by their last names, draw attention to any
extra departures from cleanliness.... There always seem to
be more of them in the room than there actually are.

❧ *Margaret Atwood*

Men choose the self and women choose others.

❧ *Mary Field Belenky, Blythe McVicker Clinchy,*
Nancy Rule Goldberger & Jill Mattuck Tarule

Just because a man's a man doesn't mean he's a natural-born
tinkerer. Many a boy grows up, in this specialized and urban age
of ours, without ever having tinkered at all.

❧ *Peg Bracken*

A lot of men think of their wives as replacing their mothers.

❧ *Joyce Brothers*

Men get opinions as boys learn to spell,
By reiteration, chiefly.

❧ *Elizabeth Barrett Browning*

Two angels decide how humans should reproduce: "If the females
have the babies, the men will feel really inferior—we'll give them
enormous egos to make up for it."

❧ *Cathy & Mo*
quoted by Regina Barreca

The male ego with few exceptions is elephantine to start with.
➧ *BETTE DAVIS*

One does *not* hug boys.
➧ *HENRIETTE DESSAULLES, AGE 14*

Men's feelings that we are not really human originate
in their infancy.
➧ *DOROTHY DINNERSTEIN*

Men know everything—all of them—all the time—no matter how
stupid or inexperienced or arrogant or ignorant they are.
➧ *ANDREA DWORKIN*

Men's men: gentle or simple, they're much of a muchness.
➧ *GEORGE ELIOT*

He was like a cock who thought the
sun had risen to hear him crow.
➧ *GEORGE ELIOT*

In the man whose childhood has known caresses and kindness, there
is always a fibre of memory that can be touched to gentle issues.
➧ *GEORGE ELIOT*

Men often marry their mothers....
➧ *EDNA FERBER*

Scratch almost any man, and you'll find wistful memories of his
mother darning socks and cooking Sunday lunch and sending his
father off in the morning with swept lapels and always, but

always, being there to support and encourage her family.
♦ *LINDA BIRD FRANCKE*

Inside every adult male is a denied little boy.
♦ *NANCY FRIDAY*

Men are unable to admit that they are wrong, no
matter how lightweight the issue.
♦ *SONYA FRIEDMAN*

Most men are like music-boxes, which you can
wind up to play their set of tunes, and then they stop;
in our society the set consists of only two or
three tunes at most. No new melodies are
added after five-and-twenty at farthest.
♦ *MARGARET FULLER*
QUOTING A FRIEND

There wouldn't be half as much fun in the world if it
weren't for children and men, and there ain't a mite of
difference between them under the skins.
♦ *ELLEN GLASGOW*

[I]t is only a boy who can force his mother into submission.
♦ *SYLVIA GREEN*

We will no longer be led only by that half of the
population whose socialization, through toys,
games, values and expectations, sanctions violence as
the final assertion of manhood, synonymous with nationhood.
♦ *WILMA SCOTT HEIDE*

All men are not slimy warthogs. Some men are silly giraffes, some
woebegone puppies, some insecure frogs. But if one is not careful,
those slimy warthogs can ruin it for all the others.

➤ CYNTHIA HEIMEL

Man has really experienced woman only as mother, loved one,
and so on, that is, always in ways related to himself.

➤ EMMA JUNG

A man has by nature the urge to understand the things
he has to deal with; small boys show a predilection
for pulling their toys to pieces to find out what
they look like inside or how they work.

➤ EMMA JUNG

Bachelor: An unmarried man who often relies on
women (mother, waitress, cleaning woman, etc.)
for help with his food preparation, housecleaning and laundry.
He is not a match for, semantically or otherwise, *spinster*.

➤ CHERIS KRAMARAE & PAULA A. TREICHLER

It's as much due to the male's ego as to his sperm
that humankind keeps on reproducing.

➤ IRMA KURTZ

All young men are world-changers, before they marry.

➤ DORIS LESSING

A man's home may seem to be his castle on the outside;
inside, it is more often his nursery.

➤ CLARE BOOTHE LUCE

Men are made in job lots like their own cravats.
> *MARY MACLANE*

HECKLER (during speech by Agnes Macphail):
Don't you wish you were a man?
MACPHAIL: Yes. Don't you?
> *AGNES MACPHAIL*
QUOTED BY ALLAN GOULD

John, after his beating me at chess has had the satisfaction of
teaching me. If he wallops me absolutely he remarks "A good
game. You're getting on." If it is a draw he exclaims "My God I'm a
complete idiot. I've lost my head completely."
This strikes me as very male.
> *KATHERINE MANSFIELD*

A man loves to come home and find his wife or his mother
darning his socks. He likes to believe that she does this joyously.
> *NELLIE MCCLUNG*

The lovely thing about being forty is that you can appreciate
twenty-five-year-old men more.
> *COLLEEN MCCULLOUGH*

[Women] are the real sportsmen.
They don't have to be constantly building up frail
egos by large public performances like
over-tipping the hat-check girl, speaking fluent
French to the Hungarian waiter, and sending back
the wine to be recooled.
> *PHYLLIS MCGINLEY*

Sons do not need you. They are always out of your reach,
Walking strange waters.
Their mouths are not made for small and intimate speech
Like the speech of daughters.
➤ *PHYLLIS MCGINLEY*

This world-wide phenomenon
(in which small boys turn away
from women, enjoy being unkempt and dirty,
and show intense hostility to girls) has
only a pallid complementary reflection
in the lives of little girls.
➤ *MARGARET MEAD*

[I]n general the masculine nature is bigger than the
feminine, more connected, and more as if it had been
made from one mold; that is probably why it is the way it is.
➤ *PAULA MODERSOHN-BECKER*

...sons forget what grandsons wish to remember....
➤ *ALICE ROSSI*

Know ye not, oh foolish ones, that a man dreadeth a female cynic
as a small boy dreadeth an education?
➤ *HELEN ROWLAND*

Men will *not* change, *unless they have to.*
➤ *DORA RUSSELL*

I like men to behave like men—strong and childish.
➤ *FRANÇOISE SAGAN*

[A man] accepts devotion as a matter of course. He regards it as
his by inherent right, for the simple reason that he came forth
from the body of Madame his mother.

    ❧ *GEORGE SAND*

It is delightful to be a woman; but every man
thanks the Lord devoutly that he isn't one.

    ❧ *OLIVE SCHREINER*

Boys are sent out into the world to buffet
with its temptations, to mingle with bad and good,
to govern and direct...girls are to dwell in quiet homes
among a few friends, to exercise a noiseless influence,
to be submissive and retiring.

    ❧ *ELIZABETH MISSING SEWELL*

The male is psychically passive.
He hates his passivity, so he projects
it onto women, defines the male as active,
then sets out to prove that he is
("prove he's a Man").... Since he's attempting to
prove an error, he must "prove" it again and again.

    ❧ *VALERIE SOLANAS*

Not only is it harder to be a man,
it is also harder to become one.

    ❧ *ARIANNA STASSINOPOULOS*

A man I used to know
Has become my child

    ❧ *ANNE SZUMIGALSKI*

...I don't think I could get along with a man.... I can see so many
things about men, rather childish, babyish things that
I'd be sure to say some sarcastic bity [sic] thing.
Men are so funny. They're so boyish—
oh well you know what I mean.
➤ *MARION TAYLOR*

Men require a lot from women, and taking care of
yourself as a person is a full-time job.... I think they ought to
become persons, and then they don't have to lean so heavily on
the female that she loses part of her life.
➤ *JOYCE CAROL THOMAS*

Gee, I get tired of hearing that boys can do a
certain thing but girls can't.
➤ *KATE TOMIBE, AGE 19*

Mercy on us, these men act like children, and badly behaved ones
at that.
➤ *JILL TWEEDIE*

War is the ultimate male ego trip.
➤ *BARBARA G. WALKER*

Men ain't got any heart for courting a girl
they can't pass—let alone catch up with.
➤ *JESSAMYN WEST*

I've never gone anywhere where the men
have come up to my infantile expectations.
➤ *DAME REBECCA WEST*

Tommy was divine last night....
When I lie back in his arms
and give him my lips I forget everything except
the sweet, gentle, greedy feel of him....
He is every inch a man, bless his inartistic soul.
 ✦ WINIFRED WILLIS

FLORRIE: I know you were secretly
hoping for a boy, but boys are such a mischief,
much more trouble to look after.
It's not such a bad thing to have all girls.
 ✦ THE WOMEN'S THEATRE GROUP

The only time a woman really succeeds in changing
a man is when he's a baby.
 ✦ NATALIE WOOD

A mature prince would never address his wife as "mother."
 ✦ MARION WOODMAN

The egotism of men surprises and
shocks me even now. Is there a woman of my
acquaintance who could sit in my armchair
from 3 to 6:30 without the semblance of a suspicion
that I may be busy, or tired, or bored;
and so sitting could talk, grumbling and grudging
of her difficulties, worries; then eat chocolates,
then read a book, and go at last, apparently
self-complacent and wrapped in a kind of
blubber of misty self-satisfaction?
 ✦ VIRGINIA WOOLF

If one didn't feel that politics are an elaborate game got
up to keep a pack of men trained for that sport in condition,
one might be dismal; one sometimes is dismal.

➤ *VIRGINIA WOOLF*

Isn't this "reputation" the deepest of all masculine instincts?

➤ *VIRGINIA WOOLF*

S E X U A L I T Y

"THEY'RE ONLY AFTER ONE THING"

Men find flagrantly sexual women taxing,
the office being demanding enough.
> ERICA ABEEL

Most men flirt to reassure themselves that they are
still attractive to the opposite sex.
> JOYCE BROTHERS

A man who insists he never has a twinge of
desire for another woman, never fantasizes about
other women, and lusts only for his wife—
after twenty years of marriage, mind you—is,
in my opinion, a phoney.
> HELEN GURLEY BROWN

Getting married to the *first* man you make
off with in an office or anywhere else is so *dull*.
You ought to sample several before you
make up your mind.
> HELEN GURLEY BROWN

The American male's breast fixation dates from
the war years of the Forties and remains
unmatched throughout the world
for obsessional fervor.
➤ SUSAN BROWNMILLER

Speaking of rapists, even the most diehard feminist
must admit that's one thing men do better than women.
➤ GABRIELLE BURTON

People [men] who are so dreadfully devoted to their
wives are so apt, from mere habit, to get devoted
to other people's wives as well.
➤ JANE WELSH CARLYLE

Men make love more intensely at twenty, but
make love better, however, at thirty.
➤ CATHERINE II OF RUSSIA

At least some of the men who write sex books admit that they
really don't understand female sexuality. Freud was one. Masters is
another—that was why he got Johnson.
➤ ARLENE CROCE

The act of sex...is man's last desperate stand at superintendency.
➤ BETTE DAVIS

We learn [in literature] of a male's attaining manhood
in sexual initiations; much less frequently of a woman's
feelings on losing her virginity.
➤ JANICE DELANEY, MARY JANE LUPTON & EMILY TOTH

NORMA: Eddy always falls dead asleep after.
MEG: Men are made different.
➤ *MAUREEN DUFFY*

He thinks because I'm flat on my back he's got me but I've got him: caught, clenched as if I had my teeth in him.
➤ *MAUREEN DUFFY*

The problem is, they have too many hormones. And they have this trouble all the time, not just ten days a month, like a woman does.
➤ *SALLY DUSTIN*

A man needs the sexual conquest to prove that he can still do it, that he can still get it up. It's like having a duel with himself. He has to prove it all the time. We don't have to prove it.
➤ *PRINCESS ELIZABETH OF YUGOSLAVIA*

A young man who grows up expecting to dominate sexually is bound to be somewhat startled by a young woman who wants sex as much as he does, and multi-orgasmic sex at that.
➤ *NORA EPHRON*

A lot of younger men are curious about what an older woman can do for them.
➤ *SANDY FAWKES*

The joy of an ardent young lover is that he wants it *now* and it doesn't matter if you are in the bathroom, the kitchen, a field, a shop doorway, or in a car, on a plane, train or building site.
➤ *SANDY FAWKES*

Most pitiful [are] the grown men who regard
women as something to burnish their egos, a mere decoration
for the end of their cock, the ones who had never
learned to enjoy women's company.

    ▶ *SANDY FAWKES*

When modern woman discovered the orgasm
it was (combined with modern birth control)
perhaps the biggest single nail in the
coffin of male dominance.

    ▶ *EVA FIGES*

Men love women at any price, love women even though,
beginning in childhood, it is the female sex which
makes the male feel guilty about what he
desires most from them.

    ▶ *NANCY FRIDAY*

A man is so constituted that he must indulge his passions or die!
(so it has been inculcated on women for centuries).

    ▶ *MARGARET FULLER*

The only place men want depth in a
woman is in her décolletage.

    ▶ *ZSA ZSA GABOR*

VI: Men have a tendency not to disapprove of rape—
that is, unless their own mother, wife,
daughter or sister are involved. When this is
the case they are liable to become...hysterical.

    ▶ *PAM GEMS*

CHRISTINA: I love men! Their company, their talk...the smell of man's sweat in the saddle! I love them in the bone...in the flesh...the wildness...the pricky insolence. The truth that is in a man takes him where his flesh decides. The flesh chooses!
> *PAM GEMS*

For men obsessed with women's underwear, a course in washing, ironing and mending is recommended.
> *CHARLOTTE PERKINS GILMAN*

I am not going to hang myself just because some wretched little man sticks his dick into me.
> *GERMAINE GREER*
> *QUOTED BY ANGELA NEUSTATTER*

A man is more than a dildo.
> *GERMAINE GREER*

The male attitude toward sex is like squirting jam into a doughnut.
> *GERMAINE GREER*

Men do not like you to leave your stockings around, men like to be managed, men do not like brassieres held together with a safety pin, and there is no lack of ravishing and smartly dressed women; men only really love you if you evade them; men always prefer a flirt who does not love them to a girl with untidy hair who adores them; you must never show a man you care for him, and you must fight on every front to be better turned out every day than the others.
> *BENOITE GROULT*

All too many men still seem to believe, in a rather naive
and egocentric way, that what feels good to them is
automatically what feels good to a woman.

➧ *SHERE HITE*

If men knew what women laughed about,
they would never sleep with us.

➧ *ERICA JONG*

There's a difference between male and female sexuality:
done and done, for the man; still ebbing, for the woman.
That's why a man can always be at least sexually satisfied,
whatever else he gets from an encounter.

➧ *ALICE KOLLER*

A man goes away when he uses up his sexual interest
in a woman, if he has no incentive to search for
other interests to share with her.

➧ *ALICE KOLLER*

BRENDA: And you know what marks off Canadian
husbands from the rest of the world? I'll tell you.
GEORGE: I thought you might.
BRENDA: A Canadian husband thinks he has achieved
the epitome of sexual prowess when he can do it in his sleep,
so he doesn't waste any time.

➧ *BETTY LAMBERT*

Men aren't attracted to me by my mind.
They're attracted by what I don't mind.

➧ *GYPSY ROSE LEE*

There's something about a man with a whacking
great erection that [is] hard to resist.
➤ *Doris Lessing*

MIRIAM: It beats me how, in a taxi, the nicest
guy turns into Harpo Marx.
➤ *Clare Boothe Luce*

A woman's a woman until the day she dies,
but a man's a man only as long as he can.
➤ *Moms Mabley*

One kind of man I impatiently scorn is the kind that looks bored
if I mention Ibsen or ceramics or Aztec civilization but is
interested instantly, alertly if I mention my garters.
➤ *Mary MacLane*

Men are those creatures with two legs and eight arms.
➤ *Jayne Mansfield*

Male sexuality seems originally focussed to no
goal beyond immediate discharge.
➤ *Margaret Mead*

Men created marriage in part to provide each male
with his own sexual object.
➤ *Barbara Mehrhof & Sheila Cronan*

Husbands are chiefly good lovers when they
are betraying their wives.
➤ *Marilyn Monroe*

One of the genuine and recurrent surprises of my life concerns the importance to men of physical sex....For me the actual performance of the sexual act seemed of secondary importance and interest. I suspect this is true for most women....
➧ *JAN MORRIS*

Men need to be de-spunked regularly.
➧ *CYNTHIA PAYNE*

Men fake too.
➧ *ALEXANDRA PENNEY*

Boys don't make passes at female smart-asses.
➧ *LETTY COTTIN POGREBIN*

It is in better taste somehow that a man should be unfaithful to his wife away from home.
➧ *BARBARA PYM*

Tell me what a man finds sexually attractive and I will tell you his entire philosophy of life.
➧ *AYN RAND*

We are still the property of men, the spoils today of warriors who pretend to be our comrades in the struggle, but who merely seek to mount us....
➧ *DIANE RAVITCH*

Good men have dogs, but order them to leave the room during love-making.
➧ *ERIKA RITTER*

No man ever stuck his hand up your dress
looking for a library card.
➤ *JOAN RIVERS*

A man can sleep around, no questions asked, but if a woman
makes 19 or 20 mistakes she's a tramp.
➤ *JOAN RIVERS*

Men mainly interested in women have had to marry or
pay or rape until quite recently.
➤ *JANE RULE*

Men, probably because they do not get pregnant,
have always been able to confront their sexual needs
as something separate from their domestic lives.
➤ *JANE RULE*

Many men simply don't understand that there are
several kinds of relationships you can have with women—
and sleeping with them, or wishing you could,
is not all there is.
➤ *MERLE SHAIN*

I prefer corncobs to the genitals of the male.
➤ *ELIZABETH SMART*

For men, the unearned reputation of sexual
activity sometimes aggrandizes social position;
for women, before very recent times, it would prove
devastating to status in respectable society.
➤ *PATRICIA MEYER SPACKS*

No man can be held throughout the day
by what happens through the night.
♦ *Sally Stanford*

Man in his lust has regulated long enough this
whole question of sexual intercourse.
♦ *Elizabeth Cady Stanton*

A man, brought up to be my opposite, was
supposed to pierce the mystery. He, the first one,
had to guide me through the unknown territory
of myself, my silenced body. His body was supposed to have
a voice. An imperative voice, capable of mastering
my alien instrument and making music!
♦ *Renate Stendhal*

A single ram could impregnate
more than fifty ewes.
With power comparable to this,
what could man not achieve?
♦ *Reay Tannahill*

Men ought to have an adoration for one,
and indeed to do everything to make up, for what
after all they alone are the cause of!
♦ *Queen Victoria*

We got new evidence as
to what motivated man to walk upright:
to free his hands for masturbation.
♦ *Jane Wagner*

When a man gets hanged, he gets an erection, but when a woman gets hanged, the *last* thing on her mind is sex.
> ❧ JANE WAGNER

A hard man is good to find.
> ❧ MAE WEST

Give a man a free hand and he'll try to run it all over you.
> ❧ MAE WEST

Some men are all right in their places—if they only knew the right places!
> ❧ MAE WEST

Wise men do not force themselves into dry loins!
> ❧ RUTH WESTHEIMER

Outside of every thin woman is a fat man trying to get in.
> ❧ KATHERINE WHITEHORN

Men don't often worry about offending women with their sexual grunts, groans, or heavy breathing, or their wondrous, noisy peeing from the heights.
> ❧ ELIZABETH FRIAR WILLIAMS

It [inarticulate passion] is the sort of thing men always feel at first, before they decide they'd rather die than marry me, and *will* die if I don't yield to their immoral demands! I often think of how few men have proposed marriage to me, and of how many have wanted me!
> ❧ WINIFRED WILLIS

It is a curious thing how the one idea of every man who comes to see me is to assume a prostrate position as speedily as possible— also to get me to do the same thing!

➤ JOAN WYNDHAM

It's terribly important to be poked by someone nice the first time. Most girls get awful men, and it puts them off poking for good.

➤ JOAN WYNDHAM

I have often thought that men who care passionately for women attach themselves at least as much to the temple and to the accessories of the cult as to their goddess herself.

➤ MARGUERITE YOURCENAR

· R E L A T I O N S H I P S ·

"FRIENDSHIP IS IMPOSSIBLE BETWEEN
A MAN AND A WOMAN"

♥

The male still gets all the fancy steps [in the mating dance].
> *ERICA ABEEL*

Liberty is a better husband than love to many of us.
> *LOUISA MAY ALCOTT*

He said to me he would be true,
And change me for none other new;
Now I sykke and am pale of hue,
For he is far.
> *ANONYMOUS, 15TH CENTURY*

Old lovers go the way of old photographs,
bleaching out gradually as in a slow bath of acid: first the moles
and pimples, then the shadings, then the faces themselves, until
nothing remains but the general outlines.
> *MARGARET ATWOOD*

Alas men are not so thrillingly absorbing as all that, except in that
fatal period of being in love.
> *MARY BERENSON*

Men friends...are shoulder to shoulder.
Female friends are more often eye to eye.
➤ *LOUISE BERNIKOW*

The Prince must be able to give the heroine something
she cannot get for herself or from other women.
➤ *LOUISE BERNIKOW*

Behind almost every woman you ever heard of
stands a man who let her down.
➤ *NAOMI BLIVEN*
QUOTED BY REGINA BARRECA

Something becomes of a man's fidelity...when he gives it to a
number of women or tries it in a number of places.
➤ *KAY BOYLE*

It has been established that men fall in love faster than women.
➤ *JOYCE BROTHERS*

Men have always been unfaithful.
➤ *JOYCE BROTHERS*

Some men stay more faithful than others because
they are not powerfully sexed.
➤ *HELEN GURLEY BROWN*

A man who might not have the nerve to ask you to dinner—
or be certain he wanted to spend an entire evening with you—
will check you out at lunch.
➤ *HELEN GURLEY BROWN*

I'd never seen men hold each other. I thought the only things
they were allowed to do was shake hands or fight.
➤ RITA MAE BROWN

Even male "losers" can find some woman to take
care of them, certainly far more easily than female "winners" can
find men or women to care for them.
➤ PHYLLIS CHESLER

Men love and fall in love romantically, women
sensibly and rationally.
➤ SURVEYS REPORTED BY NANCY CHODOROW

Men grow up rejecting their own needs for love,
and therefore find it difficult and threatening to
meet women's emotional needs. As a result, they collude in
maintaining distance from women.
➤ NANCY CHODOROW

CLIVE: Friendship between men is a fine thing.
It is the noblest form of relationship.
➤ CARYL CHURCHILL

TEN THINGS TODAY'S WOMEN LOOK FOR IN A MAN
1. Vasectomy scars
2. Intelligence
3. Time
4. A sense of humor
5. A deceased mother
6. A vase
7. A steady job with room for advancement

8. Good teeth
9. A hard body
10. Good demographics
+ *Susan Connaught Curtin & Patricia O'Connell*

The average man is more interested in a woman
who is interested in him than he is in a woman—any woman—
with beautiful legs.
+ *Marlene Dietrich*

The only men who are too young are the
ones who write their love letters in crayon, wear pajamas
with feet, or fly for half fare.
+ *Phyllis Diller*

Man and woman are two locked caskets, of which
each contains the key to the other.
+ *Isak Dinesen*

The reason husbands and wives do not understand each
other is because they belong to different sexes.
+ *Dorothy Dix*

Few men would admit to marrying for reasons other
than love or domestic incompetence.
+ *Barbara Ehrenreich & Deirdre English*

Keeping the peace with the particular man
in one's life becomes more essential than battling
the mass male culture.
+ *Susan Faludi*

You can't hang on to [young lovers]
because eventually
they have to go on with their own lives.
♦ SANDY FAWKES

Men's love of women is filled with rage.
♦ NANCY FRIDAY

[A]s long as the feminine mystique masks
the emptiness of the housewife's role...
there never will be enough Prince Charmings,
or enough therapists to break that pattern....
♦ BETTY FRIEDAN

Give a man top priority in your life—make
him the main course—and chances are you will lose
not only your self but your self-esteem.
♦ SONYA FRIEDMAN

Men should deserve a woman's love as an inheritance,
rather than seize and guard it like a prey.
♦ MARGARET FULLER

My theory is that men love with their eyes;
women love with their ears.
♦ ZSA ZSA GABOR

A man in love is incomplete
until he has married.
Then he's finished.
♦ ZSA ZSA GABOR

Many men have had casual dating relationships
with women, and perhaps a few complex love-sex
relationships, but most men have not had an
intimate non-sexual friendship with a woman.

➤ *CAROL GILLIGAN*

To hold a man, or several men, was for her the
epitome of female gamesmanship, the only
thing that made life meaningful. What war is to men.

➤ *FRANÇOISE GIROUD*

A guy who'd cheat on his wife would cheat at cards.

➤ *TEXAS GUINAN*

Marriage to a lover is fatal; lovers are not husbands. More
important, husbands are not lovers.

➤ *CAROLYN HEILBRUN*

The compulsion to find a lover and husband
in a single person has doomed more women
to misery than any other illusion.

➤ *CAROLYN HEILBRUN*

Sometimes I wonder if men and women
really suit each other. Perhaps they should live next door
and just visit now and then.

➤ *KATHARINE HEPBURN*

Really, it is all just a game, and you don't need to have an affair
with a man to have an intuitive understanding of him.

➤ *ETTY HILLESUM*

I don't need an overpowering, powerful, rich man to
feel secure. I'd much rather have a man who is there for me,
who really loves me, who is growing, who is real.

> ✦ *BIANCA JAGGER*

"Every man (said Coleridge) would like to have an Ophelia or a
Desdemona for his wife." No doubt; the sentiment is truly a
masculine one: and what was *their* fate?

> ✦ *ANNA BROWNELL JAMESON*

It is hard to fight an enemy who has outposts in your head.

> ✦ *SALLY KEMPTON*

Personally, I think if a woman hasn't met the right man by the
time she's 24, she may be lucky.

> ✦ *JEAN KERR*

For a man, a woman can be either a vessel or a friend;
for a woman, unless a man is her friend,
sex is merely a temporary connection.

> ✦ *ALICE KOLLER*

BRENDA: Men and women are natural enemies.
Natural blood enemies.
➤ *BETTY LAMBERT*

In every animal under the sun
below man (as far as I know)
it is the male who has to please the female.
Yet among men, it is the opposite.
➤ *MARTHA LAVELL*

A man stirs me because he can be my life,
the visage, the presence, the tenderness of every day,
and not because he has some sort of right of
possession and perturbation over me.
➤ *MARIE LÉNÉRU*

How can a man trust a woman who falls in love with
him only after they have made love?
➤ *DORIS LESSING*

A man has only one escape from his old self: to
see a different self—in the mirror of some woman's eyes.
➤ *CLARE BOOTHE LUCE*

MAGGIE: A man don't like to be told no
woman but his wife is fool enough to love him.
It drives 'em nutty.
➤ *CLARE BOOTHE LUCE*

Men make wounds and women bind them up.
➤ *NELLIE McCLUNG*

Men like frivolity—before marriage;
but they demand all the sterner virtues afterwards.
> *NELLIE MCCLUNG*

I think most men take a little knowing.
> *A FRIEND OF NELLIE MCCLUNG*

Any person can tell, when they look around at men in general,
that God never intended women to be very particular.
> *ANONYMOUS SUFFRAGIST*
> *QUOTED BY NELLIE MCCLUNG*

For men, giving is clearly an added luxury
that is allowed only *after* they have fulfilled the primary
requirements of manhood.
> *JEAN BAKER MILLER*

To each masquerading male the female is a mirror
in which he beholds himself.
> *KATE MILLETT*

I think I wept a lost dream—a dream that could
never be fulfilled—a girl's dream of the lover who should
be her perfect mate, to whom she might splendidly give herself
with no reservations. We all dream that dream.
And when we surrender it unfulfilled we feel that something
wild and sweet and unutterable has gone out of life!
> *LUCY MAUD MONTGOMERY*

For me, a man I have loved becomes a kind of brother.
> *JEANNE MOREAU*

Man has been defined as a woman-caressing animal,
and the definition is so absolutely correct that
it is beyond controversy.
> *EMILY GOWAN MURPHY*

The prince—I want him.
> *AZALIA EMMA PEET*

The prince doesn't come. Now and then I think I catch a glimpse
of him but I soon find out my mistake.
> *AZALIA EMMA PEET*

I want the prince to come. When will he come? Never?
> *AZALIA EMMA PEET*

Your mildest men, if they have sense, know how
to treat women of honour.
> *MARY PIX*

Old boyfriends, many women report,
make excellent cat-sitters.
> *ERIKA RITTER*

Then there's the man who says, "I'll call you....Or you call me."
Principles of equality notwithstanding, experience teaches us that
keeping things loose very soon degenerates into keeping things vague.
> *ERIKA RITTER*

Somewhere there was a gentle man with a cock that wore a jaunty
grin and stayed long enough for you to get to know him.
> *JILL ROBINSON*

[I] wonder if what makes men walk lordlike and speak so
masterfully is having the love of women.

▶ *ALMA ROUTSONG*

The average man takes all the natural taste
out of his food by covering it with ready-made sauces,
and all the personality out of a woman by covering
her with his ready-made ideals.

▶ *HELEN ROWLAND*

Men do not love women.
They use them and exploit them, and then
consider it fair to subject them to the law of fidelity.

▶ *GEORGE SAND*

I knew how bad men are,
I did not know how commonplace they are.

▶ *GEORGE SAND*

Whereas a woman's chief emotional need
is active (i.e., to love), a man's prime emotional
need is passive (i.e., to be appreciated or admired).

▶ *PHYLLIS SCHLAFLY*

Many a man thinks yelling, "Is dinner ready?"
is the same as saying "I love you."

▶ *MERLE SHAIN*

There are no perfect men of course, but some are more perfect
than others, and we can use all of those we can get.

▶ *MERLE SHAIN*

Men are not given awards and promotions for bravery in intimacy.
➤ *GAIL SHEEHY*

A man's heart is a shameful thing.
When he is with a woman whom he finds tiresome and
distasteful, he does not show that he dislikes her,
but makes her believe she can count on him.
➤ *SEI SHONAGON*

Men will walk, dear, over our broken and bleeding hearts,
but we must love them still in spite of everything.
➤ *MINNA SIMMONS*
FROM A LETTER QUOTED BY RUTH SLATE IN HER DIARY

[A friend] told me I was wrong to cherish the
romantic idea of the one man for one woman.
➤ *RUTH SLATE*

Even the love of man is only a remedy for man.
➤ *ELIZABETH SMART*

I like gentlemen friends and they like me and
there's an end'out [end to it] to me at least.
➤ *ELIZABETH SMITH*

Love is the very history of a woman's life,
it is merely an episode in a man's.
➤ *MADAME DE STAEL*

The more I see of men, the more I like dogs.
➤ *MADAME DE STAEL*

Men folks don't like to think someone likes them.
They like elusiveness.
➧ *MARION TAYLOR*

Boyfriends weren't friends at all; they were prizes,
escorts, symbols of achievement, fascinating strangers,
The Other.
➧ *SUSAN ALLEN TOTH*

The basic male tenets: men do not care to
love but are innately lovable, women love but are
not intrinsically lovable.
➧ *JILL TWEEDIE*

Men jousted with death and pretended
they did it for women.
➧ *JILL TWEEDIE*

Man is a hating rather than a loving animal.
➧ *DAME REBECCA WEST*

It is very nice, having a man in love with you.
➧ *WINIFRED WILLIS*

Men can taste unpleasant and look perfectly alarming.
Women love them anyway.
➧ *NAOMI WOLF*

When you take the penis,
you take the man who comes with it.
➧ *MARION WOODMAN*

Women have served all these centuries as looking-glasses
possessing the magic and delicious power of reflecting the figure
of man at twice its natural size.

*   *VIRGINIA WOOLF*

ALICE: Most [men] seize up and develop a terrible
shortness of breath, often for years, frequently for a lifetime,
before they are ever able comfortably to say,
"I love you," "te amo," "je t'aime"....
On the other hand, beware of a [man] who tells you
that he loves you, especially too fast, especially in
the heat of the moment.

*   *BETTY JANE WYLIE*

It is easier to get priceless jewels
Than to find a man with a true heart.

*   *YU HSUAN-CHI*

• T H E   F A M I L Y •
M A N

"A MAN'S HOME IS HIS CASTLE"

♥

I cannot say that I think you very generous to the Ladies, for whilst
you are claiming peace and good will to Men, Emancipating all
Nations, you insist on retaining absolute power over wives.

❧ *Abigail Adams*

Philosopher: A man up in a balloon, with his family and friends holding
the ropes which confine him to earth and trying to haul him down.

❧ *Louisa May Alcott*

...when two people marry they become in the eyes of the
law one person, and that one person is the husband!

❧ *Shana Alexander*
Introduction to State-by-State Guide to Women's Legal Rights, 1975

It's true, there are never any evil stepfathers.
Only a bunch of lily-livered widowers, who let me get away with
murder vis-à-vis their daughters. Where are they when I'm
[the stepmother] making those girls drudge in the kitchen,
or sending them out into the blizzard in their paper dresses?
Working late at the office. Passing the buck. Men!
But if you think they knew nothing about it, you're crazy.

❧ *Margaret Atwood*

It is a truth universally acknowledged,
that a single man in possession of a good fortune,
must be in want of a wife.
❧ *Jane Austen*

It is always incomprehensible to a man that a
woman should ever refuse an offer of marriage.
❧ *Jane Austen*

A wedding is a sort of an alarm to love,
it calls up every man's courage.
❧ *Aphra Behn*

The frequent failure of men to cultivate their
capacity for listening has a profound impact on
their capacity for parenting, for it is mothers
more than fathers who are most likely
to still their own voices so they may hear
and draw out the voices of their children.
❧ *Mary Field Belenky, Blythe McVicker Clinchy,
Nancy Rule Goldberger & Jill Mattuck Tarule*

In the present order of things
(perhaps it will always be so) in marriage
the man takes everything from the woman.
Of course he gives some things in exchange, but not all.
He absorbs *the whole* woman's life and
gives her love, support, a home, much of his
time, but not his life, in the sense
in which she gives hers.
❧ *Mary Berenson*

A household is much easier to organize
without a man in it.
+ MARY BERENSON

Whether they know it or not, men need
marriage more than women do.
+ JESSIE BERNARD

It has always been economically and politically
important for men to know that they are
the fathers of their children.
+ LOUISE BERNIKOW

When it comes to fixing something around the house, many a
modern husband is an inert mass. Perhaps this is because he
doesn't *want* to fix things. It is equally possible that he doesn't
know a faucet washer from his right foot.
+ PEG BRACKEN

The average man doesn't care much for the frozen-food
department, nor for the pizza man, nor for the
chicken-pie lady. He wants to see you knead that bread
and tote that bale, before you go down cellar to make the soap.
This is known as Woman's Burden.
+ PEG BRACKEN

Husbands, with a few grim exceptions, don't care much. They want
a modest modicum of order, that's all. They'd rather not see how it
got there, either, and they hate the whine of a vacuum cleaner only
slightly less than the wail of a policeman's siren hard behind.
+ PEG BRACKEN

Men want the same thing from their writers that they want from
their wives, a certain type of predictability.
➤ *KATE BRAVERMAN*

Men do not think
Of sons and daughters, when they fall in love....
➤ *ELIZABETH BARRETT BROWNING*

Fathers see babies as potentially grown-up—
they are more likely than mothers to transform their
perception of their newborn into fantasies about the adult it will
become, and about the things they (father and child) will be able
to do together when the infant is much older.
➤ *DOROTHY BURLINGHAM*

A man loves a woman so much, he asks her to marry—
to change her name, quit her job, have and raise the babies, be
home when he gets there, move where his job is. You can hardly
imagine what he might ask if he didn't love her.
➤ *GABRIELLE BURTON*

I think a bad husband is far worse than no husband.
➤ *MARGARET CAVENDISH, DUCHESS OF NEWCASTLE*

The thought of a husband is as terrible to me as
the sight of a hobgoblin.
➤ *SUSANNAH CENTLIVRE*

If it were natural for fathers to care for their sons,
they would not need so many laws commanding them to do so.
➤ *PHYLLIS CHESLER*

It is a habit of all men to fancy that in some inscrutable way their
wives are the cause of all the evil in their lives.

➤ *MARY BOYKIN CHESNUT*

The male is a domestic animal which, if treated with firmness and
kindness, can be trained to do most things.

➤ *JILLY COOPER*

I never married because there was no need. I have three pets at
home which answer the same purpose as a husband. I have a dog
which growls every morning, a parrot which swears all the
afternoon and a cat that comes home late at night.

➤ *MARIE CORELLI*

Men are forever guests in our homes, no matter how much
happiness they may find there.

➤ *ELSIE DE WOLFE*

One of the great reasons why so many husbands and wives make
shipwrecks of their lives together is because a man is always seeking
for happiness, while a woman is on a perpetual still hunt for trouble.

➤ *DOROTHY DIX*

I have noticed that the men who make the biggest fuss
over a little pleasure on the Sabbath are the ones
who enjoy the biggest Sunday dinners.

➤ *ALICE DUNBAR-NELSON*

Divorced men are now more likely to meet their car payments
than their child support obligations.

➤ *SUSAN FALUDI*

There's nothing on earth so savage—except a bear
robbed of her cubs—as a hungry husband.
> *FANNY FERN*

Marriage does but slightly tie men
Whilst close prisoners we remain....
> *ANNE FINCH, COUNTESS OF WINCHILSEA*

[N]ine men out of ten never actually propose to their wives,
it merely becomes an understood thing.
> *MARGARET FOUNTAINE*

Men may resist, but in the end most do
marry because they want women more than anything else;
if responsibilities, mortgages, ulcers, child care,
and monogamy are part of the package they
must buy to get women, they'll do it.
> *NANCY FRIDAY*

Twenty years ago, the family was not such a fragile
unit as it is today. A man knew who washed his socks.
> *SONYA FRIEDMAN*

Only men could be responsible for the belief that
a boy child is to be preferred to a girl child.
> *MARGARET FULLER*

The Husband with insulting Tyranny
Can have ill Manners justify'd by Law;
For Men all join to keep the Wife in awe.
> *SARAH FYGE*

Husbands are like fires. They go out when unattended.
♪ *Zsa Zsa Gabor*

A man is *so* in the way in the house.
♪ *Elizabeth Gaskell*

I've been married to one Marxist and one Fascist,
and neither one would take the garbage out.
♪ *Lee Grant*

The self-centred father never once has
his daughter's welfare in mind.
♪ *Sylvia Green*

Masculine culture contains a strong vein of anti-domesticity.
♪ *Germaine Greer*

Responsibility is the price every man must pay for freedom.
♪ *Edith Hamilton*

Husbands may require more housework than they contribute.
> *HEIDI HARTMANN*
QUOTED BY LETTY COTTIN POGREBIN

Alas! were men but half as anxious to fulfill
their own share of the engagements entered into in the most
important concern in life as they are to press home matrimonial
duties upon women, all might be well....
> *MARY HAYS*

Babies don't need fathers, but mothers do.
Someone who is taking care of a baby needs to be taken care of.
> *AMY HECKERLING*

The patriarchal marriage is a disastrous institution for both sexes.
> *CAROLYN HEILBRUN*

After the first year, husbands don't put
the seat back down any more.
> *BARBARA HOLLAND*

Fathers often use too much force.
> *JENNY HOLZER*

Men can and do make good mothers,
but not many choose to go that route.
> *MARNI JACKSON*

On the whole good husbands and faithful lovers are not *more*
common in savage than in civilized life, as far as I can learn.
> *ANNA BROWNELL JAMESON*

Any woman who still thinks marriage is a
fifty-fifty proposition is only proving that she
doesn't understand either men or percentages.
> *FLORYNCE KENNEDY*

A man should kiss his wife's navel every day.
> *NELL KIMBALL*

Many men feel free to refuse domestic
duty on the grounds that they detest it; many more
grumble constantly when they're stuck with
anything more than taking out the garbage.
> *PENNEY KOME*

Men's inclination for machine technology
does not extend to the washing machine.
> *PENNEY KOME*

Fathers are something else.
They always give up their turn by saying
something like, "Go ask your mother.
She knows about things like that."
> *MARY KUCZKIR*

The average man's expectations of a home are minimal:
warmth, food, clean shirts, not too many questions asked,
and sex when necessary.
> *IRMA KURTZ*

Why *is* it that men aren't interested in children?
> *MARTHA LAVELL*

And where
was your father all this time?
Away
at the war, or
in his office, or any-
way conspicuous for his
Absence

     ❥ LIZ LOCHHEAD

Men *can* clean, of course, but women *do* clean.

     ❥ MARY LOWNDES

MAGGIE: The first man who can think up a good explanation how
he can be in love with his wife *and* another woman is going to win
that prize they're always giving out in Sweden!

     ❥ CLARE BOOTHE LUCE

If men had to bear babies, there'd never be more
than one child in a family. And he'd be a boy.

     ❥ CLARE BOOTHE LUCE

All women contribute more to marriage than men.

     ❥ AGNES MACPHAIL

So often this week I've heard you [her husband]
and Gordon talking while I washed dishes.
Well, someone's got to wash dishes and get food.
Otherwise—"There's nothing in the house but eggs to eat."
Yes, I hate hate *hate* doing these things that you
accept just as all men accept of their women.

     ❥ KATHERINE MANSFIELD

Of course my father always said I should have
grown up to be a boy.
➧ MARIA GOEPPERT MAYER

Men just want their vittles and a lot
they care who gives it to them.
➧ NELLIE McCLUNG

The thing to remember about fathers is, they're men.
➧ PHYLLIS McGINLEY

The degeneration of the father's role
into that of a tired, often dreaded,
nightly visitor has done much to make his son's
happy identification with him impossible....
The child is forced to identify with a lay figure in trousers.
➧ MARGARET MEAD

Patriarchy's chief institution is the family.
➧ KATE MILLETT

Funny, from the very beginning of marriage
it's we women who are put to the test.
All you men are permitted
to stay simply the way you are.
Well, I don't really take
that amiss because I do like you all so very much.
➧ PAULA MODERSOHN-BECKER

Men gain more instrumentally from marriage than women do.
➧ MALKAH NOTMAN & CAROL NADELSON

If you take away a man's responsibility
to provide for his wife and children,
you've taken away everything he has.
A woman, after all, can do
everything a man can do.
And have babies.
❧ *ANN PATTERSON*
QUOTED BY JANE O'REILLY

Men fear entrapment in marriage more
than women; is this because the wife is
of the same sex as the primary
caretaker of childhood?
❧ *ETHEL SPECTOR PERSON*

Most men cannot find in their own kitchen
what most women can find in a stranger's kitchen.
❧ *LETTY COTTIN POGREBIN*

Men do not want to have to take care of children.
Rule them, yes. Play with them, yes.
Take credit for their achievements, certainly.
But not care for their bottles, diapers, mess,
spills, tears, tantrums, laundry, lunches, nightmares,
and the million daily details of childhood.
❧ *LETTY COTTIN POGREBIN*

Marriage is slavery, it prevents one from
surrendering oneself to that supreme happiness
which the initiated call love—and so I think it is.
❧ *NELLY PTASCHKINA*

I wanted to be alone, and what better place to choose than the
sink, where neither of the men would follow me?
➤ *BARBARA PYM*

Marriage is a lottery in which men stake their liberty
and women their happiness.
➤ *VIRGINIE DES RIEUX*

It isn't tying himself to one woman that a man
dreads when he thinks of marrying; it's separating
himself from all the others.
➤ *HELEN ROWLAND*

A husband is what is left of the lover
after the nerve has been extracted.
➤ *HELEN ROWLAND*

Before marriage, a man will lie awake
all night thinking about something you said;
after marriage he'll fall asleep before you finish saying it.
➤ *HELEN ROWLAND*

Husbands are like Christmas gifts:
you can't choose them; you've just got to sit down
and wait until they arrive and then appear
perfectly delighted with what you get.
➤ *HELEN ROWLAND*

Whenever I date a guy, I think, is this the man I want my children
to spend their weekends with?
➤ *RITA RUDNER*

Often one person of a couple has the talent and desire to be mate
and parent—the terms for it are martyr and saint for the female,
henpecked and castrated for the male.

> ↟ *JANE RULE*

The marriage vow is an absurdity
imposed by society.

> ↟ *GEORGE SAND*

Married men are like the balls on Bollo-bats soaring
high off the horizon secured by an invisible string.

> ↟ *MERLE SHAIN*

As for those who say, "yes, dear, whatever
you say, dear," while doing exactly as they please—
they are the worst there is.

> ↟ *MERLE SHAIN*

All the stories about husbands taking out the garbage and
minding the children are really diversionary tactics.

> ↟ *CATHERINE SHIFF*

[A friend] says she thinks a man unsatisfactorily married suffers
and hungers more than a woman because a woman can find
comfort in the depths of another woman, but very seldom a man
in another man—and sex is the barrier to prevent
him finding it in another woman.

> ↟ *EVA SLAWSON*

Every man who marries has found his natural protector.

> ↟ *HANNAH WHITALL SMITH*

Patriarchy is based on the appropriations
of women's bodies and energy by men.
+ *DALE SPENDER*

Many men in the blind gratification of their passions force
excessive maternity on women and...this is likely to continue so
long as man continues to write, speak and act as if maternity were
the one and sole object of a woman's existence.
+ *ELIZABETH CADY STANTON*

Common is the man who will permit his aged mother to carry
pails of water and armfuls of wood, or his wife to lug a twenty
pound baby, hour after hour, without ever offering to relieve her.
+ *ELIZABETH CADY STANTON*

A man might have a harem if he chose, and if he
could defend it, but the concept of "my" son requires the woman
to be monogamous.
+ *REAY TANNAHILL*

Many men resent any inkling that their wives want
to get them to do things.
+ *DEBORAH TANNEN*

I'll not have a hub [husband].
There [*sic*] awful bothers anyway.
+ *MARION TAYLOR*

I wish my husband had a greater influence on me. It is strange that I
should love him so terribly and yet feel his influence so little.
+ *SOPHIA TOLSTOY*

As for my incomparably more gifted husband!
What extraordinary understanding of people's psychology
in his writings, and what incomprehension and
indifference to the lives of those closest to him!
➤ SOPHIA TOLSTOY

The father, no matter how good...
a father cannot keep the family intact.
➤ ANNA F. TREVISAN

The idea of being protected by men dies hard...we all,
in varying degrees, decreasing with age, cherished some small
hope of the idyllic warmth of male shelter.
➤ ANNE TRUITT

No man is responsible for his father.
That is entirely his mother's affair.
➤ MARGARET TURNBULL

Daddy is a Daddy, after all,
and likes to be amused
after a long day or even smack a
naughty bum, in his wisdom.
➤ JILL TWEEDIE

Bess says 'tis a woman's place to keep the
house for the gentleman and see to his comfort.
That is what marriage is for. I'm thinking there's
more than that to it or the ladies would not
be so forward about it.
➤ MAGGIE OWEN WADELTON, AGE 12

Almost nothing of any value was ever done by a man who had to take care of his own household and cookery, not to mention child care and other mundane chores of daily life.

➤ *Barbara G. Walker*

A man in the house is worth two on the street.

➤ *Mae West*

If men's love for women and for their own children led them to define themselves first as fathers and lovers, the propaganda of war would fall on deaf ears.

➤ *Naomi Wolf*

The *divine right* of husbands, like the divine right of kings, may, it is hoped, in this enlightened age, be contested without danger.

➤ *Mary Wollstonecraft*

It has been predicted that by the year 2000 all the poor in the United States will be women and their children. What happens to men's children?

➤ *Betty Jane Wylie*

· T H E   W O R K I N G ·
M A N

"MAN WORKS FROM SUN TO SUN"

♥

All the men on my staff can type.
BELLA ABZUG

Men work to achieve goals. Women work to prevent catastrophe.
BERIT AS
QUOTED BY PENNEY KOME

Men's novels are about how to get power.
Killing and so on, or winning and so on.
MARGARET ATWOOD

Yes, yes, if you please, no reference to examples in books. Men
have had every advantage of us in telling their own story.
Education has been theirs in so much higher a degree; the pen has
been in their hands. I will not allow books to prove anything.
JANE AUSTEN

A man would never get the notion of writing a book on the
peculiar situation of the human male.
SIMONE DE BEAUVOIR

A man's indebtedness...is not virtue; his repayment is.
➧ *Ruth Benedict*

Whether he admits it or not,
a man has been brought up to look at money
as a sign of his virility, a symbol of his power,
a bigger phallic symbol than a Porsche.
➧ *Victoria Billings*

No matter how much men may complain about the tab,
most men want to pick it up because of the fringe benefits
that go with paying the expenses.
➧ *Victoria Billings*

Men are men and women are women
and their paychecks are just further
evidence of their vast biological differences,
the powerful influence of the X and Y chromosomes.
➧ *Mary Kay Blakely*

Men are not opposed to women working,
just against their being paid for it.
➧ *Barbara Bodichon*

Men judge us by the success of our efforts,
God looks at the efforts themselves.
➧ *Charlotte Brontë*

The men who hate career girls hate
the career girls who hate *men.*
➧ *Helen Gurley Brown*

The feeling is that until men are comfortable working in some of these fields that are traditionally considered to be female...women end up doing two jobs, and the men are still doing just one.

➧ *ROSEMARY BROWN*

What I love about the men's work is its celebration.

➧ *JANET BURROWAY*

If housework is so fulfilling,
why aren't men beating down the doors to get in on it?

➧ *GABRIELLE BURTON*

Men painters mostly despise women painters.

➧ *EMILY CARR*

The men resent a woman getting any honour in what they consider is essentially their field.

➧ *EMILY CARR*

Progress is the prerogative of men; even the male lifestyle is based on the premise of uninterrupted progress.

➧ *ANNA COOTE & BEATRIX CAMPBELL*
QUOTED BY DALE SPENDER

The fact that most gynecologists are males is itself a colossal comment on "our" society.

➧ *MARY DALY*

The power of money is a distinctly male power. Money speaks, but it speaks with a male voice.

➧ *ANDREA DWORKIN*

There are no laws requiring
husbands to buy life-insurance policies.
➧ *Barbara Ehrenreich*

The more a woman earns or expects to earn,
the easier it is for a man to leave with a clear conscience.
➧ *Barbara Ehrenreich*

Male culture seems to have abandoned the
breadwinner role without overcoming the sexist attitudes
that role has perpetuated: on the one hand, the expectation of
female nurturance and submissive service as a matter of right;
on the other hand, a misogynist contempt for
women as "parasites" and entrappers of men.
➧ *Barbara Ehrenreich & Deirdre English*

"We men are the breadwinners," say the sentimentalists, who are
ashamed of their female relatives appearing to work, though
female earnings usually drop into men's pockets.
➧ *Englishwoman's Journal, July 1, 1858*

Housework's the hardest work in the world.
That's why men won't do it.
➧ *Edna Ferber*

Providing for one's family as a good husband
and father is a water-tight excuse for making money hand
over fist. Greed may be a sin, exploitation of other people
might, on the face of it, look rather nasty, but who can
blame a man for "doing the best" for his children?
➧ *Eva Figes*

Our society forces boys, insofar as it can,
to grow up, to endure the pains of growth, to
educate themselves to work, to move on.

> ♦ *BETTY FRIEDAN*

A man may feel frustrated when a woman
shows that she is as proficient as he in an
area he considers his own territory.

> ♦ *SONYA FRIEDMAN*

We [Sarah and Emily] commenced to pick
raspberries at 11 A.M. & quit at 7 P.M. sold...30 qts.
total worth $2.40 for 14 hrs. work...per hour...would be
.438 while a man would want & get
$2.00 for same time, *Equality*.

> ♦ *EMILY GILLESPIE*

To a wife, her husband is her food supply.

> ♦ *CHARLOTTE PERKINS GILMAN*

She gets her living by getting a husband.
He gets his wife by getting a living.

> ♦ *CHARLOTTE PERKINS GILMAN*

These are hard times for men, for they
are losing their servants.

> ♦ *CHARLOTTE PERKINS GILMAN*

The comfort a man takes with his wife
is not in the nature of a business partnership.

> ♦ *CHARLOTTE PERKINS GILMAN*

Men can cook, clean, and sew as well as women,
but the making and managing of the great engines
of modern industry, the threading of earth and
sea in our vast systems of transportation, the
handling of our elaborate machinery of trade, commerce,
government—these things could not be done
so well by women in their present
degree of economic development.

➤ *CHARLOTTE PERKINS GILMAN*

The labor of women in the house, certainly,
enables men to produce more wealth than
they otherwise could; and in this way
women are economic factors in society.
But so are horses.

➤ *CHARLOTTE PERKINS GILMAN*

Man, too, pays his toll,
but as his sphere is wider,
marriage does not limit him
as much as woman.
He feels his chains more
in an economic sense.

➤ *EMMA GOLDMAN*

It's these downscale men,
the ones who can't earn as much as
their fathers, who we find are the most
threatened by the women's movement.

➤ *SUSAN HAYWARD*
QUOTED BY SUSAN FALUDI

The only jobs for which no man is qualified
are human incubator and wet nurse.
Likewise, the only job for which no woman
is or can be qualified is sperm donor.
➤ *WILMA SCOTT HEIDE*

Success isn't everything but it makes a man stand straight.
➤ *LILLIAN HELLMAN*

Men see work as a series of tasks to be completed,
all adding up to something; women often
look at a job as an endless stream of work,
with no beginning, middle or end.
➤ *MARGARET HENNING & ANN JARDIN*

There is only one other profession
that outranks bankers as dedicated clients,
and that is the stockbroker....
When the stocks go up, the cocks go up!
➤ *XAVIERA HOLLANDER*

Is not the tremendous strength in men of
the impulse to creative work in every field precisely due
to their feeling of playing a relatively small part in the
creation of living beings, which constantly impels
them to an overcompensation in achievement?
➤ *KAREN HORNEY*

After all, a man don't ask much. He wants his dinner, he wants
clean socks, what's wrong with that?
➤ *INTERVIEW QUOTED BY JANE HOWARD*

The assumption of a male-breadwinner society...ends up determining the lives of everyone within a family, whether a male breadwinner is present or not, whether one is living by the rules in suburbia or trying to break them on a commune.

> ❥ *Louise Kapp Howe*

Men own 99 percent of the world's property and earn 90 percent of its wages, while producing only 55 percent of the world's food and performing only one-third of the world's work.

> ❥ *Statistics taken from an International Labor Organization study presented at the United Nations Women's Conference in Copenhagen, 1980*

Most men have been raised to be utterly passive to the female world of the home—the thought that men *make* a home is still, alas, a novel one.

> ❥ *Marni Jackson*

Behind every man who achieves success
Stand a mother, a wife and the IRS.

> ❥ *Ethel Jacobson*

A friend's report: "The men are much alarmed by certain speculations about women." Her comment: "And well they may be, for when the horse and ass begin to think and argue, adieu to riding and driving."

> ❥ *Anna Brownell Jameson*

Automation and unions have led to a continuously shortened day for men but the work day of housewives with children has remained constant.

> ❥ *Beverly Jones*

There are very few jobs that actually require a penis or a vagina. All other jobs should be open to everybody.

♦ *FLORYNCE KENNEDY*

Chances are better than even that if you ask the nearest man, he'll cheerfully tell you that housework is not work.

♦ *PENNEY KOME*

Men cook for business, or to show off.

♦ *IRMA KURTZ*

Nine times out of ten when a man is altruistic it's a tax dodge.

♦ *IRMA KURTZ*

Women understand that men must often be kept from soiling themselves with the dirty details of life in order to accomplish the big shiny jobs unimpeded. And women in politics have generally accepted this role—to do all the hum-drum, tedious, must-be-done jobs.

♦ *JUDY LAMARSH*

GEORGE: Not that I'm against equal rights for women. I'm all for equal rights, equal voting privileges, equal working conditions. I have submitted a White Paper urging the desegregation of the university bathrooms. It's just that I don't think women should make as much money as us real people.

♦ *BETTY LAMBERT*

At some point in history, the male took control of the female's industry, probably because he realized that the pasture was more profitable than the hunting ground.

♦ *ANN J. LANE*

Men will work their fingers to the bone for women—
but not with them.

➤ *NELLIE McCLUNG*

Men fought because they liked it;
and women worked because it had to be done.

➤ *NELLIE McCLUNG*

Man long ago decided that woman's sphere was anything
he did not wish to do himself, and as he did not particularly care
for the straight and narrow way, he felt free to recommend it to
women in general. He did not wish to tie himself too close to
home either and still he knew somebody should stay on the job,
so he decided that home was woman's sphere.

➤ *NELLIE McCLUNG*

If women may not work in mines,
why should men be allowed to paint teacups?

➤ *LADY McLAREN*

Men who appear far more favored and more free than their
women-folk have not yet reached the level of self-realization that
would have been theirs had their wives and mothers also had
roles that they could attain and enjoy.

➤ *MARGARET MEAD*

Male society recognizes as activity only what men do.

➤ *JEAN BAKER MILLER*

No modest man ever did or will make a fortune.

➤ *LADY MARY WORTLEY MONTAGU*

No *man*, not even a doctor, ever gives any other definition of what a nurse should be other than this—"devoted and obedient." This definition would do just as well for a porter. It might even do for a horse. It would not do for a policeman.

➤ *FLORENCE NIGHTINGALE*

Only when men are connected to large, universal goals are they really happy—and one result of their happiness is a rush of creative activity.

➤ *JOYCE CAROL OATES*

Men will always opt for things that get finished and stay that way—putting up screens, but not planning menus.

➤ *JANE O'REILLY*

The man has the burden of the money. It's needed day after day. More and more of it. For ordinary things and for life. That's why holidays are a hard time for him. Another hard time is the weekend, when he's not making money or furthering himself.

➤ *GRACE PALEY*

To tell a woman using her mind that she is
thinking with a man's brain means telling her that she can't
think with her own brain; it demonstrates your
ineradicable belief in her intellectual inadequacy.

❧ *FRANÇOISE PARTURIER*

Behind every successful man stands a surprised woman.

❧ *MARYON PEARSON*

To the old saying that man built the house but woman made of it
a "home" might be added the modern supplement that woman
accepted cooking as a chore but man has made of it a recreation.

❧ *EMILY POST*

...before long I should be certain to find myself at
his sink peeling potatoes and washing up; that would be a nice
change when both proof-reading and indexing began to pall.
Was any man worth this burden? Probably not, but one
shouldered it bravely and cheerfully.....

❧ *BARBARA PYM*

Men want recognition of their work, to help them to believe in
themselves.

❧ *DOROTHY MILLER RICHARDSON*

A man at his desk in a room with a closed door is a man at work.
A woman at a desk in any room is available.

❧ *BETTY ROLLIN*

Never mind how many women are out there working. The
workplace is still, for the most part, owned and run by men, and

we're there because they've allowed us to be there—
sometimes because they *had* to—and we know it and
they know it and they know we know it.
➤ *BETTY ROLLIN*

The fact is that men still do rather consistently undervalue or
devalue women's powers as serious contributors to civilization
except as homemakers.
➤ *MAY SARTON*

Women in literature written by men are so rarely great *persons*.
➤ *MAY SARTON*

What men are against is women obtaining jobs which are pleasant,
exciting and profitable and which they wish to reserve for themselves.
➤ *DOROTHY SAYERS*

I wondered why the birth of a child appealed so little to the
imagination of the artist. Why were all the great realistic novels of
the world concerned with only one aspect of sex?
➤ *EVELYN SCOTT*

Fathers are present as absences in family life. Who really had a father?
Even people who did have fathers didn't. Men were working.
➤ *MONA SIMPSON*

When a woman has been down on her knees scrubbing for a
week, and washing for another week, a man, returning and
finding his house in order, and vaguely conscious of a newer and
fresher smell about it, talks quite tenderly of "a woman's touch."
➤ *MAY SINCLAIR*

A man can always command his time under the plea of business; a woman is not allowed any such excuse.

♦ *Mary Somerville*

Under the traditional sexual division of labour the tunnel vision of males is reinforced. They do not see what every woman knows.

♦ *Dale Spender*

...no man can call himself liberal, or radical, or even a conservative advocate of fair play, if his work depends in any way on the unpaid or underpaid labor of women at home, or in the office.

♦ *Gloria Steinem*

I have yet to hear a man ask for advice on how to combine marriage and a career.

♦ *Gloria Steinem*

Men thought it natural for women to do all the boring, repetitive, or onerous chores that they themselves didn't want to do; but for women to do something interesting or intellectually stimulating was viewed as a violation of the divine order.

♦ *Barbara G. Walker*

The world goes on singing the praises of the pioneer, the "man who opens the door." Could he open it if the woman did not hand him the key? Not from what I have seen.

♦ *Mary Schaeffer Warren*

He should have put his wife to work. That's the way doctors and lawyers pay for their education nowadays.

♦ *Jessamyn West*

Whatever women do they must do twice as well as men to be thought of as half as good. Luckily, this is not difficult.

> ❧ *CHARLOTTE WHITTON*

We men have nothing to fear. Women can't qualify for our good jobs since we deprive them of the necessary training.

> ❧ *JOYCE WOOD*

To men, money is a game.
If you don't believe me, watch any man play Monopoly.

> ❧ *BETTY JANE WYLIE*

Studies reveal that a man can be jealous of his wife's work, particularly if she makes more money than he does—fortunately for him, this doesn't happen very often.

> ❧ *BETTY JANE WYLIE*

The best couturiers, hairdressers, home designers and cooks are men. I suspect that were it biologically possible men would make better mothers.

> ❧ *IDA ALEXA ROSS WYLIE*

· C O M M U N I C A T I O N ·
B E T W E E N   T H E
S E X E S

"THEY JUST DON'T SPEAK THE SAME LANGUAGE"

Father had conversations. Mother took boarders.

♥ *LOUISA MAY ALCOTT*

Fie on the falsehood of men, whose minds go oft a madding,
and whose tongues can not so soon be wagging,
but straight they fall a railing.

♥ *JANE ANGER*

The desire that every man has to show his true vein in writing is
unspeakable, and their minds are so carried away with the
manner, as no care at all is had of the matter.

♥ *JANE ANGER*

A man's true ideas are those he lives by,
not always those he talks about.

♥ *ANONYMOUS*

When I find a guy who asks, "How was your day?" and really
wants to know, I'm in heaven.

♥ *ANONYMOUS WOMAN*
INTERVIEWED BY DEBORAH TANNEN

Man forgives woman anything save the wit to outwit him.
➤ *MINNA ANTRIM*

It is very strange that men cannot behave like rationall [*sic*] beings.
➤ *MARTHA BALLARD*

Men read the woman's funny, ironic, and sometimes
even sarcastic text as straight ("Oh, you're so strong.
Can you really crush that beer can?") and are delighted
to meet a woman who can finally "appreciate" them.
➤ *REGINA BARRECA*

The reason most men feel comfortable making jokes
directed at women is that they do not expect any viable retort.
➤ *REGINA BARRECA*

Affectation hath always had a greater share both in the actions and
discourse of men than truth and judgment have; and...I dare to
say I know of none that write at such a formidable rate, but that a
woman may well hope to reach their greatest heights.
➤ *APHRA BEHN*

The man who can't understand why women can't
be more like men is the same man who will
complain if women change their behavior.
➤ *VICTORIA BILLINGS*

There's a difference between the sexes
where canapes are concerned. Women like them pretty
and men usually just don't like them.
➤ *PEG BRACKEN*

Men readily interrupt the speech of women,
and women allow the interruption.

> ❧ *Susan Brownmiller*

Trading baseball statistics, discussing
the physical attributes of women or negotiating deals is
considered appropriate conversation among men,
and being tightmouthed about information
that others can use to their advantage is
considered a masculine virtue.

> ❧ *Susan Brownmiller*

Language conceals an invincible adversary
because it's the language of men and their grammar.

> ❧ *Hélène Cixous*

What is man, when you come to think upon him,
but a minutely set, ingenious machine for turning,
with infinite artlessness, the red wine of Shiraz into urine?

> ❧ *Isak Dinesen*

Ritual verbal gang-banging is so staple
an ingredient of ordinary respectable man-to-man
conversation that any objection to it is taken as a tasteless assault
on an inoffensive form of pleasantry.

> ❧ *Dorothy Dinnerstein*

A man is entitled to issue blunt orders,
contradict people flatly, instruct or command
or forbid outright, without apology or circumlocution.

> ❧ *Dorothy Dinnerstein*

Leave the opinions of men to their natural perversity—their actions are the best test of their faith.

➤ *MARIA EDGEWORTH*

What man can prevail upon himself to debate three hours about what could be as well decided in three minutes?

➤ *MARIA EDGEWORTH*

Blessed is the man who, having nothing to say, abstains from giving wordy evidence of the fact.

➤ *GEORGE ELIOT*

Men are bewildered by what it is their wives are trying to tell them.

➤ *ANNA FORD*

Just as more and more women were getting paid for using their brains, more and more men represented them in novels, plays, and poems as nothing but bodies.

➤ *SANDRA M. GILBERT & SUSAN GUBAR*
QUOTED BY SUSAN FALUDI

My research suggests that men and
women may speak different languages that
they assume are the same, using similar words
to encode disparate experiences of self
and social relationships.

➤ *CAROL GILLIGAN*

For one man to own and dominate a great paper or a group of
papers is more insidiously dangerous than to have him
dominate railroads, churches, or armed men.

➤ *CHARLOTTE PERKINS GILMAN*

No man of any grade can get the social stimulus
he needs by spending every evening with his cook!...
you may love her dearly, but you are not
satisfied with her conversation.

➤ *CHARLOTTE PERKINS GILMAN*

Very few men who have slept around
casually are able to converse humanely
with the women who have extended their favours.

➤ *GERMAINE GREER*

Men trivialize the talk of women not
because they are afraid of any such talk, but in
order to make women themselves downgrade it.

➤ *CAROLYN HEILBRUN*

Men are frightened by women's humor, because they think when
women are alone, they're making fun of men.

➤ *NICOLE HOLLANDER*

Men have always detested women's gossip because they suspect
the truth: their measurements are being taken and compared.

➤ *ERICA JONG*

Throughout all of history, books were
written with sperm, not menstrual blood.

➤ *ERICA JONG*

[Men] have assimilated the misogyny of male humor,
and with some guilt they expect that feminist
humor will return their treatment in kind.

➤ *GLORIA KAUFMAN*

A man speaks only when driven to speech by something outside
himself—like, for instance, he can't find any clean socks.

➤ *JEAN KERR*

Men have more say in mixed-sex interaction;
they are more likely to treat women as conversation
pieces rather than as conversationalists. Because women spend
more time listening and observing than men who control,
women hear and see things men do not.

➤ *CHERIS KRAMARAE & PAULA A. TREICHLER*

A sense of humour is a sturdy companion to
the human spirit. Isn't it a crying shame so few men have one?

➤ *IRMA KURTZ*

[A]fter seeing nothing but young men for so long,
it is quite a treat to converse with a middle-aged one.

➤ *ANNE LANGTON*

Let men enjoy in peace and triumph the intellectual kingdom
which is theirs, and which doubtless was intended for them.
> *SARAH LEWIS*

When a man can't explain a woman's actions, the first thing he
thinks about is the condition of her uterus.
> *CLARE BOOTHE LUCE*

A Good Scout is the sort of man who if a woman
trusts him with one one-hundredth of her heart will take the
whole heart and twist and batter it and read the paper and smoke
his pipe and pay the bills: serenely unaware.
> *MARY MACLANE*

Men feel more pressured to cut short their receptiveness and to
rush to put forward their own reactions. Often they clearly
betray the fact that they have not received
or heard much of what the other was communicating.
> *JEAN BAKER MILLER*

Men are always ready to respect anything that bores them.
> *MARILYN MONROE*

I discovered that even now men
prefer women to be less informed, less able, less talkative,
and certainly less self-centred than they are themselves;
so I generally obliged them.
> *JAN MORRIS*

In polite society women do most of the talking. This is not
because men are stupid but by reason of the fact that clothes and

scandal may be mentioned in polite society, while money
and stomachs are subjects tabooed.

❧ *Emily Gowan Murphy*

This is courtship all the world over—
the man all tongue; the woman all ears.

❧ *Emily Gowan Murphy*

Men, who can not participate in the whole process of reproductive
labor, are alienated and they have needed to seek other kinds of
creativity—such as abstract thought and political life—
to create a continuity of their own.

❧ *Mary O'Brien*

I am assuming that what men watch and read and write is nobler
than what women watch. Baseball is not nobler.

❧ *Jane O'Reilly*

Though men may be deep, mentally they are slow.

❧ *Camille Paglia*

Still, if we were back at the table, I'd probably have to talk to him.
Look at him—what could you say to a thing like that? Did you go
to the circus this year, what's your favorite kind of ice cream, how
do you spell cat? I guess I'm as well off here. As well off as if I
were in a cement mixer in full action.

❧ *Dorothy Parker*

You men can't stand the truth, sir, as soon as
it embarrasses your interest or your pleasure....

❧ *Françoise Parturier*

[I] wonder how it happened that so many different men—and learned men among them—have been and are so inclined to express both in speaking and in their treatises and writings so many wicked insults about women and their behavior.

➤ *CHRISTINE DE PIZAN*

Men's fears and beliefs about their women are remarkably standard; I know a number of men who've accused their wives of being cheats, whores, sluts. Most of those women never looked at another man. And yet none of those husbands would have been certified insane.

➤ *HELEN FOGWILL PORTER*

Good men show no inclination in the world to talk about computers, unless it's to ask a woman to explain how the damn thing works.

➤ *ERIKA RITTER*

JULIA: They never listen to what you're saying, they just want to listen to the music of your voice.

➤ *CHRISTIANE ROCHEFORT*

Men do not wish to be shown for what they are, nor to be made to laugh at the masks they have assumed.

➤ *GEORGE SAND*

There are no father-in-law jokes.

➤ *BERNICE SANDLER*

Very few men care to have the obvious pointed out to them by a woman.

➤ *MARGARET BAILLIE SAUNDERS*

Literary men, when they like women at all,
do not want literary women. What they want is girls.
* MURIEL SPARK

Men have convinced women to remain backstage so that only they
have the limelight—and then they have dared to assert that their
presence front stage proves their superiority and its divine origin!
* DALE SPENDER

Male silence is not the same as listening.
* GLORIA STEINEM

Men don't tell enough details.
* DEBORAH TANNEN

Men interrupt women.
* DEBORAH TANNEN

Men frequently annoy women by usurping or switching the topic.
* DEBORAH TANNEN

Many men have little use for small talk.
* DEBORAH TANNEN

I have learned valuable information. I have learned that the
discussion of the cultural value of history and kindred topics will
not get one very far, no matter how clever and apparently serious-
minded the gentleman may be. I have learned that one must talk
vivaciously, and on such subjects as foot-ball. One must laugh and
talk about trivial and foolish things.
* MARION TAYLOR, AGE 17

The ubiquitous nature of masculine images of Woman has
contributed significantly to the struggles of woman artists because
that which is publicly acceptable art does not conform with
their own needs and experiences, and their own
art does not conform with popular standards.

➤ *ANNE TUCKER*

[J]ust as women find uncomfortable the negative images of
themselves found in male literature, so men find it difficult to
appreciate accusations that they occupy the role of oppressor.

➤ *NANCY WALKER*

The greater the influence of men over a particular medium at a particular
time, the more traditional and outdated the images have been.

➤ *KATHRYN WEIBEL*

Any student of history knows that it is the story of men.

➤ *KATHRYN WEIBEL*

Men are so accustomed to being flattered in books
by women that simple honesty comes as a shock and
they register [it] as biased and unfair.

➤ *FAY WELDON*

The true male never yet walked
Who liked to listen when his mate talked.

➤ *ANNA WICKHAM*

A king is always a king—and a woman always a woman: his authority
and her sex ever stand between them and rational converse.

➤ *MARY WOLLSTONECRAFT*

· V U L N E R A B I L I T Y ·

"BOYS DON'T CRY"

❤

More men are talking about more feelings than at any time in recent history.

♦ *JANE ADAMS*

Energy is more attractive than beauty in a man.

♦ *LOUISA MAY ALCOTT*

When a man has a great sorrow, he should be indulged in all sorts of vagaries till he has lived it down.

♦ *LOUISA MAY ALCOTT*

Some men are not scared. They are 1) gay, 2) married.

♦ *ANONYMOUS*
Ms. *MAGAZINE LETTER*

Women have got to make the world safe for men since men have made it so darned unsafe for women.

♦ *LADY NANCY ASTOR*

Men favour heroes who are tough and hard: tough with men,
hard with women. Sometimes the hero goes soft
on a woman but this is always a mistake.

> ❯ *MARGARET ATWOOD*

What men are most afraid of is not lions, not snakes,
not the dark, not women. Not any more. What men are most
afraid of is the body of another man. Men's bodies are the most
dangerous things on earth.

> ❯ *MARGARET ATWOOD*

Men's bodies are detachable. Consider the history of statuary:
the definitive bits get knocked off so easily, through
revolution or prudery or simple transportation, with leaves
stuck on for substitutes, fig or grape; or, in more northern
climates, maple. A man and his body are soon parted.

> ❯ *MARGARET ATWOOD*

A man is two people, himself and his cock. A man always
takes his friend to the party. Of the two, the friend is nice,
being more able to show his feelings.

> ❯ *BERYL BAINBRIDGE*

No man needs curing of his individual sickness;
his universal malady is what he should look to.

> ❯ *DJUNA BARNES*

It is perhaps difficult to prove scientifically that men cannot truly
laugh at a joke told by a woman and maintain an erection, but an
informal survey of both men and women indicates that it's so.

> ❯ *REGINA BARRECA*

Men ceased weeping when it became unfashionable.
> *SIMONE DE BEAUVOIR*

...no one is more arrogant toward women, more aggressive or scornful, than the man who is anxious about his virility.
> *SIMONE DE BEAUVOIR*

Men are as afraid of us as we are of them, although few men are willing to say so. (Disclosing state secrets is treason.)
> *VICTORIA BILLINGS*

Castration fear: inevitable in a species that has knock-offable external dangling genitalia....
> *BEATA BISHOP*

Are men afraid we will mock them?
> *RITA MAE BROWN*

What fractures me about most men is that they can't live without male approval.
> *RITA MAE BROWN*

Most men expect women in general to keep male secrets, cherish male frailty, forgive male cruelty; women in general to assuage male insecurity and loneliness; women in general to provide them with some comfort, some immediate validation of themselves.
> *PHYLLIS CHESLER*

CLIVE: A boy has no business having feelings.
> *CARYL CHURCHILL*

Men, the very best of men, can only suffer,
while women can endure.
- *Dinah Mulock Craik*

If men put from them in fear all that is "womanish" in them,
then long, of course, for that missing part in their natures,
so seek to possess it by possessing us; and because
they have feared it in their own souls seek, too,
to dominate it in us—seek even to slay it—well,
we're where we are now, aren't we?
- *Barbara Deming*

Men, too, both fear and long for what will happen
when women can really say what they want.
- *Dorothy Dinnerstein*

...beware of men who cry. It's true that men who cry are sensitive
to and in touch with feelings, but the only feelings they tend to be
sensitive to and in touch with are their own.
- *Nora Ephron*

Tell me, how can a normal man get up in
the morning knowing that in an hour or a minute he may
no longer be there? How can he walk through heaps of
decomposing corpses and then sit down at the table and calmly
eat a roll? How can he defy nightmare-like risks and then be
ashamed of panicking for a moment?
- *Oriana Fallaci*

Men often wonder what it is they have done wrong.
- *Anna Ford*

Men do have a general interest in,
and anxiety about,
the size of their penises.
> *ANNA FORD*

The things I particularly like about
men are their differentness, their simplicity,
their cleverness, their ability to amuse and re-tell life
better than it is, their sense of fun, their intelligence,
their dependence on women, their boyishness—
even childishness—their ability to devote
themselves single-mindedly to their interests,
their charm, their insecurity, their character and,
above all, when they reveal it, their gentleness
and vulnerability.
> *ANNA FORD*

The hardest thing for a man to do
is to cope with feelings—his, yours,
or anyone else's—so heaven forbid that
you might confront him with the
bad news that he's hurt you.
> *SONYA FRIEDMAN*

The wisest and greatest men
are ever the most modest.
> *MARGARET FULLER*

Gentleness, it would appear,
is no asset to man.
> *LIN GREEN*

Probably the only place where a man can feel really
secure is in a maximum security prison,
except for the imminent threat of release.
➧ *GERMAINE GREER*

How rash to assert that man shapes his own destiny.
All he can do is determine his inner responses.
➧ *ETTY HILLESUM*

A man may be as much a fool from the
want of sensibility as the want of sense.
➧ *ANNA BROWNELL JAMESON*

Show me a woman who doesn't feel
guilty and I'll show you a man.
➧ *ERICA JONG*

White middle-class American males
always think that everything is someone else's problem.
➧ *MADONNA KOLBENSCHLAG*

Insecurity, boredom, fatigue, fear and distraction can all prevent
any man from an erection; apparently fidelity cannot do as much.
➧ *IRMA KURTZ*

It was so much easier for a man to *look* masculine when women
were subservient. A man didn't have to be a real man at all, and he
could fool everybody, including himself....He played a role, and
no one ever really knew or thought about what he was or felt
beneath the surface of that role.
➧ *EDA LESHAN*

Men prefer these living dolls to real women out of fear.
> *ELIZA LYNN LINTON*

[Men] know that somewhere feeling and knowledge are
important, so they keep women around to do their feeling for
them, like ants do aphids.
> *AUDRE LORDE*

Men are subconsciously afraid of women!
> *NELLIE McCLUNG*

WHY WE OPPOSE VOTES FOR MEN
1. Because man's place is in the armoury.
2. Because no really manly man wants to settle any question
otherwise than by fighting about it.
3. Because if men should adopt peaceable methods
women will no longer look up to them.
4. Because men will lose their charm if they step out of their
natural sphere and interest themselves in other
matters than feats of arms, uniforms and drums.
5. Because men are too emotional to vote. Their conduct
at baseball games and political conventions shows this,
while their innate tendency to appeal to force renders them
peculiarly unfit for the task of government.
> *ALICE DUER MILLER*

Male culture has built an amazingly large mythology around the
idea of feminine evil—Eve, Pandora's box, and the like. All this
mythology seems clearly to be linked to *men's* unsolved problems,
the things *they* fear they will find if they open Pandora's box.
> *JEAN BAKER MILLER*

In all masculine love, if you care to look, you will see
the same fickle, instinctive, passionate form of egotism
usually designated as jealousy.

♦ EMILY GOWAN MURPHY

Male attitudes toward menstruation have been primarily
negative. Blood is associated with injury, and
the menstrual blood can activate castration anxiety.

♦ MALKAH NOTMAN & CAROL NADELSON

I wonder why men can get serious at all. They have
this delicate long thing hanging outside their bodies
which goes up and down by its own will.... If I were a man
I would always be laughing at myself.

♦ YOKO ONO

Man is not merely the sum of his masks.

♦ CAMILLE PAGLIA

All men want is approval and maintenance, day after day after day.

♦ CAMILLE PAGLIA

That the most intelligent, discerning and learned men, men of
talent and feeling, should finally put all their pride in their crotch,
as awed as they are uneasy at the few inches sticking out in front
of them, proves how normal it is for the world to be crazy....

♦ FRANÇOISE PARTURIER

Fear of impotence is perhaps the
most crippling fear that a man can face.

♦ ALEXANDRA PENNEY

Size is a big issue with men.
Erection is the great equalizer.
➤ *ALEXANDRA PENNEY*

Most men have heard or read that it's not
necessary to have an erection to "satisfy" a woman,
but in their heart of hearts they don't believe it.
➤ *ALEXANDRA PENNEY*

Those men who have attacked women
out of jealousy are those wicked ones
who have seen and realized that many women
have greater understanding and are more noble
in conduct than they themselves and
thus they are pained and disdainful. Because of this,
their overweening jealousy has prompted them to
attack all women, intending to demean and diminish
the glory and praise of such women.
➤ *CHRISTINE DE PIZAN*

An emotional man may possess no humor,
but a humorous man usually has deep pockets of emotion,
sometimes tucked away or forgotten.
➤ *CONSTANCE ROARKE*

Male eschatology combines male womb
envy with womb negation.
➤ *ROSEMARY RADFORD RUETHER*

Why do some men find unsmiling women so threatening?
➤ *KAREN SAWITZ*

Penises are kind of a pain because
they're so vulnerable hanging out there like that
and men are so concerned about the way they hang
out there like that.

> ❧ *LIBBY SCHEIER*

We do not often live with the superior side of the man—that is
generally expressed in his work—but more habitually with his
weak, tired, shadow side. We indulge him, restore him, and though
we exploit him (that is a mutual game) it often seems to us our role
and fate to deal with his inferiority, and conceal it from him.

> ❧ *FLORIDA SCOTT-MAXWELL*

Condoms should be marketed in three sizes, because the failures
tend to occur at the extreme ends of the scale. In men who are
petite, they fall off, and in men who are extremely well-endowed,
they burst.... I think if it would help condom efficiency,
we should package them in different sizes, and maybe label them
like olives: jumbo, colossal, and super-colossal, so that men don't
have to go in and ask for the small.

> ❧ *BARBARA SEAMAN*
> *AT HEARINGS BEFORE THE SELECT COMMITTEE ON POPULATION, MARCH 1978*

Nice guys can't get cabs.

> ❧ *MERLE SHAIN*

Men really have strange emotions and behave in the most bizarre ways.

> ❧ *SEI SHONAGON*

I envied men. Not their bodies, everything else.

> ❧ *RENATE STENDHAL*

But men have more to them than their false image.
They've got a whole culture to protect them from
knowing about their inadequacy. They've found excellent
ways to make women bear it for them.

♦ *RENATE STENDHAL*

Men do not need to develop their emotional faculties, they are
already hideously overdeveloped.

♦ *JILL TWEEDIE*

Every man has an Achilles heel,
located not on his foot but in his crotch.

♦ *BARBARA G. WALKER*

Men resent women because women bear kids, and seem to have
this magic link with immortality that men lack. But they should
stay home for a day with a kid; they'd change their minds.

♦ *TUESDAY WELD*

They (men) like to be heroes.

♦ *FAY WELDON*

No nice men are good at getting taxis.

♦ *KATHERINE WHITEHORN*

When novelist Margaret Atwood asked women what they feared
most from men, they replied, "We're afraid they'll kill us."
When she asked men the same question about women,
they replied, "We're afraid they'll laugh at us."

♦ *REPORTED BY NAOMI WOLF*

THE RIGHT TO RULE
TO RULE

"IT'S A MAN'S WORLD"

♥

All Men would be tyrants if they could.

♪ *ABIGAIL ADAMS*

I am more and more convinced that man is a dangerous creature;
and that power, whether vested in many or a few, is ever grasping,
and, like the grave, cries, "Give, give!"

♪ *ABIGAIL ADAMS*

Never forget that a man is a selfish being. Keep that little fact in
view continually; and if you want to please him,
pander to it. Don't cry, don't make a fuss, and certainly don't
be quick-tempered. Be sweet above all, but your sweetness
must be *real*. A man never wants to be controlled.

♪ *ANONYMOUS, LATE 19TH CENTURY*

If all men are born free, how is it that all women are born slaves?

♪ *MARY ASTELL*

We've often thought men would be
easier to control if they were smaller.
> *MARGARET ATWOOD*

The male brain, now, that's a different matter. Only a thin
connection. Space over here, time over there, music and
arithmetic in their own sealed compartments. The right brain
doesn't know what the left brain is doing. Good for aiming,
though, for hitting the target when you pull the trigger. What's the
target? Who's the target? Who cares? What matters is hitting it.
That's the male brain for you. Objective.
> *MARGARET ATWOOD*

If it's natural to kill, why do men
have to go into training to learn how?
> *JOAN BAEZ*

The idea of women having power is unnerving to many men.
> *REGINA BARRECA*

Men may be cruelly exploited and subjected to all sorts of
dehumanizing tactics on the part of the ruling class, but they have
someone who is below them—at least they're not women.
> *FRANCES M. BEAL*

How is it that this world has always belonged to the men...?
> *SIMONE DE BEAUVOIR*

A man's secret fear is that a woman
will dominate him—unless he dominates her.
> *VICTORIA BILLINGS*

Male power is most forceful not as an imposition of
will but as a determinant of values.
➤ *Harriet Blodgett*

Even in the privacy of (these) very personal diaries, women honor
the formalities of male dominance by not referring to a husband
by his given name until well into the nineteenth century.
➤ *Harriet Blodgett*

Let Greeks be Greeks, and Women what they are,
Men have precedency, and still excell [sic].
➤ *Anne Bradstreet*

To envision a Chinese nobleman's wife or courtesan with daintily
slippered three-inch stubs in place of normal feet is to understand
much about man's violent subjugation of women.
➤ *Susan Brownmiller*

Through all the ages of the world's history
the more powerful sex has been liable to use their power
carelessly, not for protection only, but for pain.
➤ *Josephine Butler*

Masculine culture may occasionally be willing to allow power to a
woman if she is willing to sacrifice the qualities that make her
distinctively a woman.
➤ *Kim Chernin*

One of the great advantages to men, in a culture they dominate, is
the ability to assign to those they oppress whatever it is they wish
to disown or ignore in their own condition.
➤ *Kim Chernin*

Men, not women, are the deadliest killers of men on earth.

> ✦ *Phyllis Chesler*

With *men* it is on to the field—"glory, honour, praise, & power."
Women can only stay at home—& every paper reminds us that
women are to be *violated*—ravished & all manner of humiliation.

> ✦ *Mary Boykin Chesnut*

Just as footbinding was required by the men of China, so is
mindbinding a universal demand of patriarchal males....

> ✦ *Mary Daly*

The history of mankind is a history of repeated injuries and
usurpations on the part of man toward woman, having in direct
object the establishment of an absolute tyranny over her. To prove
this, let facts be submitted to a candid world.

> ✦ *Declaration of Sentiments and Resolutions, Seneca Falls, New York, July 1848*
> *(A convention held by women to discuss their social,*
> *civil and religious condition and rights.)*

One would think you men were lords of the universe and that we
had to go down on bended knee to get you to smile!

> ✦ *Henriette Dessaulles, age 14*

Most men—even most men who believe in principle that this
"right" is unfounded—cling hard to their right to rule the world.

> ✦ *Dorothy Dinnerstein*

The value of the penis lies mainly not in its charm as a water toy,
or in its magic erectile properties, but rather in the social
prerogatives it confers.

> ✦ *Dorothy Dinnerstein*

Police and court data indicate that
women are much more likely to be seriously assaulted or
murdered by men known to them.
* *R.E. Dobash & R. Dobash*

Man, in conquering nature, conquered the female, who had
worked with nature, not against it, to produce food and to
reproduce the human race.
* *Roxanne Dunbar*

Wars are made by old men,
fought by young men, and suffered by
women and children. Mine own epigram.
* *Alice Dunbar-Nelson*

Male dominance is the environment we know,
in which we must live.
* *Andrea Dworkin*

If men can run the world, why can't
they stop wearing neckties? How intelligent is it
to start the day by tying a little noose around your neck?
* *Linda Ellerbee*

Only a man could instigate the idea that a
woman's happiness lies in serving and pleasing a man.
* *Margaret Fuller*

Only a man could take prostitution, which is degrading for
women, and call this civilization.
* *Margaret Fuller*

Macho does not prove mucho.

♦ *ZSA ZSA GABOR*

VI: Not all rape is neurotic. Military rape occurs when men,
emerging from battle, having killed and risked death in a sexually
over-excited condition, have a profound instinct to make contact
with life, in however brutal a way. The dangerous period for
women is about six hours after combat.

♦ *PAM GEMS*

When a man lays his hands hold of his wife & Children I think tis
time something was done.

♦ *EMILY GILLESPIE*

The lust for power and conquest, natural
to the male of any species, has been fostered in him to an
enormous degree by this...cheap and easy lordship.

♦ *CHARLOTTE PERKINS GILMAN*

To the male mind an antagonist is essential to progress,
to all achievement.

♦ *CHARLOTTE PERKINS GILMAN*

War: a social disease, freely admitted to be
most characteristic of the male. It is the instinct
of sex-combat, overdeveloped and misused.

♦ *CHARLOTTE PERKINS GILMAN*

Seems nothing draws men together
like killing other men.

♦ *SUSAN GLASPELL*

Once, power was considered a masculine attribute.
In fact power has no sex.
❧ KATHERINE GRAHAM

Most men desire women who can be shown off to the boys,
women desired by other men, although evidently subjugated to
the desire for their owners alone.
❧ GERMAINE GREER

It is no small irony that, while the very social fabric
of our male-dominated culture denies
women equal access to political, economic and
legal power, the literature, myth and humor
of our culture depict women not only as
the power behind the throne, but the real
source of the oppression of men.
❧ SUSAN GRIFFIN

Chivalry is an age-old protection
racket which depends for its existence on rape.
❧ SUSAN GRIFFIN

James Bond alternately whips out his
revolver and his cock, and though there
is no known connection between the
skills of gunfighting and lovemaking,
pacifism seems suspiciously effeminate.
❧ SUSAN GRIFFIN

Men have planned everything their own way.
❧ MARY HAYS

Like many men who are compulsively cruel to
their womenfolk, he also shed tears at the cinema,
and showed a disproportionate concern for insects.
➤ *SHIRLEY HAZZARD*

Why is every gain women make followed by a fearful step
backward into the shadow of male protection?
➤ *CAROLYN HEILBRUN*

What woman does and should envy is male destiny.
➤ *CAROLYN HEILBRUN*

What would the world be like without men? Free of crime and
full of fat, happy women.
➤ *NICOLE HOLLANDER*

Men have laid down the rules and definitions by which the world
is run, and one of the objects of their definitions is women.
➤ *SALLY KEMPTON*

Men define intelligence, men define usefulness,
men tell us what is beautiful, men even tell us what is womanly.
➤ *SALLY KEMPTON*

The more macho a man is, the more of a frog he is.
➤ *MADONNA KOLBENSCHLAG*

We have long known that rape has been a way of terrorizing us
and keeping us in subjection. Now we also know that we have
participated, although unwillingly, in the rape of our minds.
➤ *GERDA LERNER*

VANDELOPE: You know what little
macho shits grow into? Big macho shits.
➤ *ALISON LYSSA*

Men who use terrorism as a means to
power, rule by terror once they are in power.
➤ *HELEN MACINNES*

Why do men go so easily to war—for we may as well admit that
they do go easily? There is one explanation. They like it!
➤ *NELLIE MCCLUNG*

The culture consents to believe the
possession of the male indicator, the testes,
penis, and scrotum, in itself characterizes
the aggressive impulse, and even vulgarly
celebrates it in such encomiums
as "that guy has balls."
➤ *KATE MILLETT*

Male supremacy, like other political creeds, does not finally reside
in physical strength but in acceptance of a value system
which is not biological.

➤ *Kate Millett*

A strong man doesn't have to be dominant toward a woman.
He doesn't match his strength against a woman
weak with love for him. He matches it against the world.

➤ *Marilyn Monroe*

Men that have not sense enough
to show any superiority in their arguments,
hope to be yielded to by a faith that,
as they are men, all the reason that has
been allotted to humankind has fallen to their share.

➤ *Lady Mary Wortley Montagu*

It makes sense that men should be comets.
They always have a following: lots and
lots of women, children, all sorts of people,
changes, crises, telephone wires.

➤ *Maryse Pelletier*

Have you ever wondered why there are so many men in the
"right-to-life" movement and so few in child care?

➤ *Letty Cottin Pogrebin*

Man's unique reward, however, is that while animals survive by
adjusting themselves to their background, man survives by
adjusting his background to himself.

➤ *Ayn Rand*

Vain creature, you do not want a woman who knows how to forgive, you want a woman who pretends to believe that you have never done anything that needs forgiveness. You want her to caress the hand that strikes her and kiss the mouth that lies to her.

❧ *GEORGE SAND*

These masterful men are like
gnarled oaks whose exterior is repellent.

❧ *GEORGE SAND*

I have had my belly full of great men (forgive the expression).
I quite like to read about them in the pages of Plutarch,
where they don't outrage my humanity. Let us see them
carved in marble or cast in bronze, and hear no
more about them. In real life they are nasty creatures,
persecutors, temperamental, despotic, bitter and suspicious.

❧ *GEORGE SAND*

Power! Did you ever hear of men being asked whether other souls
should have power or not? It is born in them.

❧ *OLIVE SCHREINER*

I still do not see why men feel such a need to stress
[the inferiority of women]. We are galled by it,
even distorted by it, mortified for them and forever puzzled.
They have gifts and strengths we lack, achievement
has been theirs, almost all concrete accomplishment
is theirs, so why do they need to give us this
flick of pain at our very being, we who are
their mates and their mothers?

❧ *FLORIDA SCOTT-MAXWELL*

How shameful when a man seduces some helpless Court lady
and, having made her pregnant, abandons her without caring in
the slightest about her future!

➤ *Sei Shonagon*

The very fact that man has the *power* to *deny* the vote to woman is
conclusive proof not only that he is in material authority, but that
he does not so recognise her right to freedom!

➤ *Eva Slawson*

Because men have power, they have the power to keep it.

➤ *Dorothy Smith*

..."the male's normal method of compensation
for not being female, namely, getting his Big Gun off,
is grossly inadequate, as he can get it off
only a very limited number of times;
so he gets it off on a really massive scale,
and proves to the entire world that he's a man.

➤ *Valerie Solanas*

It is men, not women,
who control knowledge.

➤ *Dale Spender*

Since we fear others will do to us the harm
we have done to them, men fear women
will deprive them of power, which since
history is located in the penis, hence men
have fantasies of vaginas as castrating mouths.

➤ *Una Stannard*

Though woman needs the protection of one
man against his whole sex, in pioneer life, in
threading her way through a lonely forest, on the highway,
or in the streets of the metropolis on a dark night, she sometimes
needs, too, the protection of all men against this one.

➤ *ELIZABETH CADY STANTON*

Perhaps men should think twice
before making widowhood our only path to power.

➤ *GLORIA STEINEM*

If men could menstruate,
the power justifications would go on and on.

➤ *GLORIA STEINEM*

In a patriarchy, a poor man's house may be his castle,
but even a rich woman's body is not her own.

➤ *GLORIA STEINEM*

In the pastoral society, man was dominant,
and woman as much his chattel as the
beasts he herded. It is no coincidence that the
male-oriented society of the West today should be
in a direct line of moral and philosophical descent from a few
tribes of Hebrew nomads, or that of modern India
from the Indo-European pastoralists of the *Rig-Veda*.

➤ *REAY TANNAHILL*

One of the things being in politics has
taught me is that men are not a reasoned or reasonable sex.

➤ *MARGARET THATCHER*

Growing up white and male in this
society is like swimming in a salt lake—
no matter how rotten you are, it's
impossible to sink to the bottom.
> ❧ *Sheila Tobias*

Men here are as savage as giant vipers,
And strut about in armour, snapping their bows.
> ❧ *Ts'ai Yen*

If man injures man, the injured has a great portion of power to
defend himself, either from natural strength of body, of [or?]
resolution, of [or?] the countenance of many of his fellows, or
from the laws; but when man injures woman, how can she defend
herself?...She has no hope from law; for man, woman's enemy,
exercises, as well as makes those laws.
> ❧ *Ellen Weeton*

Men, indeed, appear to me to act in a very unphilosophical
manner, when they try to secure the good conduct of women by
attempting to keep them always in a state of childhood.
> ❧ *Mary Wollstonecraft*

PEGGY: They should have a curfew for men.
Then women would be safe on the streets.
> ❧ *Betty Jane Wylie*

· THE DOUBLE· STANDARD

"SAUCE FOR THE GOOSE IS SAUCE FOR THE GANDER"

♥

Male sex drive, without an object of its affections, is a widely acknowledged fact of life, respectable even, catered to in the best neighbourhoods. But female sex drive without an object is not nearly so acceptable as today's verbal egalitarianism might suggest.

♦ *Erica Abeel*

...the men that are the most opposed to wimmin's havin' a right, and talk the most about its bein' her duty to cling to a man like a vine to a tree, they don't want Betsey to cling to them, they *won't let* her cling to 'em ...says I to 'em, "Which had you ruther do, let Betsey Bobbet cling to you or let her vote?" and they would every one of 'em quail before that question.

♦ *Samantha Allen*

According to civil law, women are equal to men. But I have to go to a religious court as far as personal affairs are concerned. Only men are allowed to be judges there—men who pray every morning to thank God He did not make them women. You meet prejudice before you open your mouth.

♦ *Shulamit Aloni*

What type of man would accept the totally liberated woman?
I am sure the answer is one who has complete confidence in
himself and sees a woman as no ego threat.

> ✦ *Anonymous*
> Ms. *magazine letter*

A doctor pointed out that estrogen (the female hormone) is at its
lowest level during the menstrual cycle. So at our "worst," we are
most like the way men are all the time.

> ✦ *Anonymous*
> North suburban *Chicago* NOW *newsletter*

Do you not see that so long as society says a
woman is incompetent to be a lawyer, minister or doctor,
but has ample ability to be a teacher, that every man of
you who chooses this profession tacitly acknowledges
that he has no more brains than a woman?

> ✦ *Susan B. Anthony*

A Man ought no more to value himself for
being wiser than a Woman, if he owes his Advantage
to a better Education, than he ought to boast of his Courage for
beating a Man when his hands were bound.

> ✦ *Mary Astell*

As for those who think so contemptibly of such
a considerable part of GOD's creation as to suppose that we were
made for nothing else but to admire and do them service,
and to make provisions for the low concerns of an animal life, we
pity their mistake and can calmly bear their scoffs,
for they do not express so much contempt of us as

they do of our Maker; and therefore the reproach of such incompetent judges is not an injury but an honor to us.
➤ *Mary Astell*

Where men tell jokes, women tell stories.
➤ *Regina Barreca*

Men say they love independence in a woman, but they don't waste a second demolishing it brick by brick.
➤ *Candice Bergen*

Man represents us, legislates for us, and now holds himself accountable for us! How kind in him, and what a weight is lifted from us! We shall no longer be answerable to the laws of God or man, no longer be subject to punishment for breaking them, no longer be responsible for any of our doings.
➤ *Amelia Jenks Bloomer*

[A] man usually gets faster results than a woman does when calling a repair firm. There is something about the deeper voice, I believe, that works better. Any man who is handy will do—the milkman, if he stops in about the time the washer conks out, or the middle-aged paper boy—just so he has a resonant baritone.
➤ *Peg Bracken*

Even those men who believe strongly in equality for women find it disturbing. No one likes to lose age-old comforts and privileges.
➤ *Joyce Brothers*

Would it upset men if they found out we weren't different?
➤ *Rita Mae Brown*

We pay veterans' benefits to soldiers
for killing, but nothing to women
who give life and sustain it.
➤ *GABRIELLE BURTON*

In this age of feminist assertion men
are drawn to women of childish body and
mind because there is something less
disturbing about the vulnerability and
helplessness of a small child—and something
truly disturbing about the body and
mind of a mature woman.
➤ *KIM CHERNIN*

Men commit actions;
women commit gestures.
➤ *PHYLLIS CHESLER*

We are told that men protect us, that they
are generous, even chivalric in their protection.
Gentleman, if your protectors were women, and
they took all your property and your children, and
paid your help half as much for your work, though
as well or better done than your own, would you
think much of the chivalry which permitted you to sit
in street-cars and picked up your pocket handkerchief?
➤ *MARY BARR CLAY*

Real men are not intimidated by women
who drive faster or more expensive cars than they do.
➤ *SUSAN CONNAUGHT CURTIN & PATRICIA O'CONNELL*

I have seen on the faces of some men who are on the whole quite likable a certain smile that I confess I find deeply unattractive: a helpless smile of self-congratulation when some female disadvantage is referred to. And I have heard in their voices a tone that is equally unattractive: a tone of self-righteous, self-pitying aggrievement when some male disadvantage becomes obvious.

> ❧ *DOROTHY DINNERSTEIN*

Men pay a heavy price for their reluctance to encourage self help and independent resources in women.

> ❧ *GEORGE ELIOT*

The real problem...is not that men are little boys but that men don't like women very much, can't deal with their demands, their sexuality, their equality.

> ❧ *NORA EPHRON*

Nothing seems to crush the masculine petals more than a bit of feminist rain—a few drops are perceived as a downpour.

> ❧ *SUSAN FALUDI*

When a man gets up to speak, people listen then look. When a woman gets up, people *look*; then, if they like what they see, they listen.

> ❧ *PAULINE FREDERICK*

Strange, isn't it? that when a man expresses a conviction fearlessly, he is reported as having made a trenchant and forceful statement, but when a woman speaks thus earnestly, she is reported as a lady who has lost her temper.

> ❧ *JESSIE B. FREMONT*

The coincidental sexual emancipation of American men—
the lifting of the veil of contempt and degradation from sexual
intercourse—was surely related to the American male's new regard
for the American woman as an equal, a person like himself,
and not just a sexual object.
➧ *Betty Friedan*

We appreciate nonsense from men
and praise them for the
very things we find inexcusable in ourselves
and in other women.
➧ *Sonya Friedman*

There is not one man, in the million, shall I say?
no, not in the hundred million, can rise above the belief that
Woman was made *for Man*.
➧ *Margaret Fuller*

The reason [a man] cannot recognise the humanity of woman is
that his own definition of the fully human is himself, and he
therefore cannot make sense of woman's differences except by
labelling them as signs of disqualification or defiance.
➧ *Matilda Joslyn Gage*

Male energy tends to scatter and destroy,
female to gather and construct.
➧ *Charlotte Perkins Gilman*

Legitimate sex-competition brings out
all that is best in man.
➧ *Charlotte Perkins Gilman*

It was all right for the young men I knew...to write about the
hymens they had broken, the diner waitresses they had seduced.
Those experiences were significant. But we were not to write
about our broken hearts, the married men we loved disastrously,
about our mothers or our children....Our desire to write about
these experiences only revealed our shallowness; it was suggested
that we would, in time, get over it.
> ♦ *MARY GORDON*

A man has only one aim in life. A woman has three, all contradictory.
> ♦ *BENOÎTE GROULT*

How great in some parts of their conduct, and how insignificant
upon the whole, would men have women to be!
> ♦ *MARY HAYS*

Since men do not take women's rights seriously,
most women also refuse to do so.
> ♦ *CAROLYN HEILBRUN*

We still have these double standards where the emphasis
is all on the male's sexual attitudes—that it's OK for him
to collect as many scalps as he can before he settles down and
"pays the price." If a woman displays the same attitude, all the
epithets that exist in the English language are laid at her door, and
with extraordinary bitterness.
> ♦ *GLENDA JACKSON*

You see an awful lot of smart guys with dumb women,
but you hardly ever see a smart woman with a dumb guy.
> ♦ *ERICA JONG*

When men imagine a female uprising they
imagine a world in which women rule men as men have
ruled women: their guilt, which is the guilt of every ruling class,
will allow them to see no middle ground.

❧ *SALLY KEMPTON*

If men could get pregnant, abortion would be a sacrament.

❧ *FLORYNCE KENNEDY*

Maybe more men than women can hoist heavy weights or pour
molten steel, but there are no muscles in the human brain.

❧ *ALICE KOLLER*

The scorn men express for a male who does housework is
exceeded only by their aversion to a woman who doesn't.

❧ *PENNEY KOME*

Men can be made attractive by scars that would ruin a woman.

❧ *IRMA KURTZ*

Aren't there superior men to like superior women?

❧ *MARTHA LAVELL*

I am beginning to see the other side of the question.
It isn't just that women want their rights; it's that they want men
to have theirs, after all these years. I figure a man has just as much
right to a seat as I have. He shouldn't have to spend his money on
a woman when she spends none on him. He shouldn't have to
earn the family's living any more than she. But neither should she
have to bring the children up any more than he.

❧ *MARTHA LAVELL*

I remember last year an hon. member who spoke from the opposite benches called a woman angel and in the next breath said that men were superior. They must therefore be gods.

♦ *AGNES MACPHAIL*

When I hear men talk about women being the angel of the home I always shrug my shoulders in doubt. I want absolute equality.

♦ *AGNES MACPHAIL*

That seems to be the haunting fear of mankind—that the advancement of women will sometime, someway, someplace, interfere with some man's comfort.

♦ *NELLIE MCCLUNG*

These tender-hearted and chivalrous gentlemen who tell you of their adoration for women, cannot bear to think of women occupying public positions...these positions would "rub the bloom off the peach," to use their own eloquent words....It is the thought of women getting into comfortable and well-paid positions which wrings their manly hearts.

♦ *NELLIE MCCLUNG*

When men cook, cooking is viewed as an important activity; when women cook, it is just a household chore.

♦ *MARGARET MEAD*

Men believe that what they do
is more important, and in this respect
they are in touch with the socially defined reality.
  ❧ JEAN BAKER MILLER

When men write about the family,
they're thought to be using it as a
metaphor for something larger.
Women, on the other hand, are seen
as writing domestic soap opera.
  ❧ SUE MILLER

Now he saw that she understood entirely
too well and he felt the usual masculine
indignation at the duplicity of women.
Added to it was the usual masculine disillusionment
in discovering that a woman has a brain.
  ❧ MARGARET MITCHELL

When men are oppressed, it's tragedy.
When women are oppressed, it's tradition.
  ❧ BERNADETTE MOSALA

There are not many males, black or white,
who wish to get involved with a woman
who's committed to her own development.
  ❧ ELEANOR HOLMES NORTON

When Harvard men say they have
graduated from Radcliffe, then we've made it.
  ❧ JACQUELINE KENNEDY ONASSIS

Men have also protected women. Men have given women
sustenance. Men have provided for women. Men have died to
defend the country for women. We must look back and
acknowledge what men have done *for women.*
> ❧ CAMILLE PAGLIA

Why is it that man's blood-shedding militancy is applauded
and women's symbolic militancy punished with a prison
cell and the forcible feeding horror...? [Men] have decided that
it is entirely right and proper for men to fight for their liberties
and their rights, but that it is not right and proper
for women to fight for theirs.
> ❧ EMMELINE PANKHURST

A woman's ass is a man's business,
but a man's ass is his business and his alone.
> ❧ MARYSE PELLETIER

In late twentieth-century America, men are more concerned than
women that their children adopt "proper"—that is, dictated,
traditional sex-role behavior.
> ❧ EVELYN PITCHER

It may have been simply my misfortune to
encounter men whose only concept of freedom was their own.
> ❧ JANE RULE

When men talk about defense, they always claim to be
protecting women and children, but they never ask
the women and children what they think.
> ❧ PAT SCHROEDER

A man who insists that his woman lay
her head on his shoulder and lean on him,
doesn't realize that if she takes her feet off the
ground in this position and hangs on she will be a drag.

➤ *MERLE SHAIN*

I earn and pay my own way as a great many women do today.
Why should unmarried women be discriminated against—
unmarried men are not.

➤ *DINAH SHORE*

Why was everything nice he did
for me a bribe or a favor, while my
kindnesses to him were my duty?

➤ *ALIX KATES SHULMAN*

Men have systematically robbed women of their
resources and have engaged in practices of distortion and
deception with regard to women and our ideas....
This treatment of women is the standard. That men may not
recognize it is their limitation.

➤ *DALE SPENDER*

A man may brave opinion; a woman must submit to it.

➤ *MADAME DE STAEL*

It is only too obvious that a man has no obligation
whatever to a woman who is considered brilliant.
To such a woman a man can be ungrateful, treacherous,
and even mean, and no one will think of taking her side.

➤ *MADAME DE STAEL*

The laws of morality seem to be suspended
in the case of relations between men and women;
a man passes off as good even though he may have
inflicted great pain upon a fellow creature,
so long as she is a woman.

♦ *MADAME DE STAEL*

Did it ever enter the mind of man that woman
too had an inalienable right to life, liberty and the
pursuit of her individual happiness?

♦ *ELIZABETH CADY STANTON*

To think that all in me of which my father would
have felt proper pride had I been a man, is deeply mortifying to
him because I am a woman.

♦ *ELIZABETH CADY STANTON*

Women age, but men mature.

♦ *GLORIA STEINEM*

Today, the male averages a higher score than
the female in tests of spatial ability (the ability to see,
hold, and adapt images in the mind), and two
American scientists have recently succeeded in
establishing an association between this ability and
certain of the basic skills of hunting, including judgment of
distance and accuracy in throwing. It is an ability
that is genetically sex-linked in a way that implies
that it must have conferred an advantage that
worked primarily through the male.

♦ *REAY TANNAHILL*

A man has to be Joe McCarthy to be called ruthless.
All a woman has to do is put you on hold.
➤ MARLO THOMAS

Society's double behavioral standard for women
and for men is, in fact, a more effective deterrent
than economic discrimination because it is
more insidious, less tangible. Economic
disadvantages involve ascertainable amounts,
but the very nature of societal value judgments
makes them harder to define,
their effects harder to relate.
➤ ANNE TUCKER

If men could give birth, then birth would now be an even more
prestigious affair than it was in the ancient matriarchies, attended
by the same cultural huzzahs that now accompany reaching the
top of a mountain, crossing the North Pole, or wiping out an
enemy machine gun nest.
➤ BARBARA G. WALKER

Ugliness is forgivable in men, but not in women.
➤ BARBARA G. WALKER

When men say "we," when they think of themselves as peers who
are in some sense equal, they do not include women in this "we";
woman remains "the absolute Other, without reciprocity."
➤ MARY ANNE WARREN

Every man I meet wants to protect me. Can't figure out what from.
➤ MAE WEST

The two sexes mutually corrupt and improve each other.

> ❧ *MARY WOLLSTONECRAFT*

A man is designed to walk three miles in the rain
to phone for help when the car breaks down—
and a woman is designed to say, "You took your time"
when he comes back dripping wet.

> ❧ *VICTORIA WOOD*

A woman...is expected to regard it as a compliment
to be told that she is in any respect the equal of a man;
I do not know how many times in my life I have been
graciously informed that I have a masculine brain.

> ❧ *BARONESS BARBARA WOOTTON*

Men are taught to apologize for their weaknesses,
women for their strengths.

> ❧ *LOIS WYSE*

A G I N G

"A MAN IS AS OLD AS HE FEELS"

♥

Ill-nature sticks to him from his youth to his gray hairs,
and a boy that's humorous [moody] and proud, makes a
peevish, positive, and insolent old man.
♪ *MARY ASTELL*

By fifty, a man may be at the peak of his career—
with power and status. A woman is washed up.
♪ *VICTORIA BILLINGS*

They [men] age earlier. But they wrinkle later.
♪ *JOYCE BROTHERS*

Men and women do not approach the dinner
table from a position of equality until they reach old age,
when the metabolic differences taper off.
♪ *SUSAN BROWNMILLER*

Old men are like that, you know. It makes them feel important to
think they're in love with somebody.
♪ *WILLA CATHER*

Love? For whom? An old man?
How horrible. For a young man? How shameful.
➧ *COCO CHANEL*

The seniority system keeps a handful of old men,
many of them southern whites hostile to
every progressive trend, in control of the Congress.
These old men stand implacably across
the paths that could lead us toward a better future.
➧ *SHIRLEY CHISOLM*

Old men's eyes are like old men's memories;
they are strongest for things a long way off.
➧ *GEORGE ELIOT*

The discovery now being celebrated
by men in mid-life of the importance of intimacy,
relationships, and care is something that
women have known from the beginning.
➧ *CAROL GILLIGAN*

I wonder if everyone, or anyone, really
thinks that forty-year-old men are "gorgeous" in
comparison to forty-year-old women. Is a man's bald
head any more attractive than a woman's graying one?
Is a man's potbelly sexier than a woman's flabby thighs?
➧ *SUSAN JACOBY*

The reason some men fear older women is
they fear their own mortality.
➧ *FRANCES LEAR*

Time comes when every man's got to feel something new—when
he's got to feel young again, just because he's growing old.
  ❧ *CLARE BOOTHE LUCE*

Men have been known to vote for years after they were dead!
  ❧ *NELLIE MCCLUNG*

But the fruit that can fall without shaking,
Indeed is too mellow for me.
  ❧ *LADY MARY WORTLEY MONTAGU*

Men may mature, but women age.
  ❧ *CYNTHIA S. POMERLEAU*

When men reach their sixties and retire, they go to pieces.
Women just go right on cooking.
  ❧ *GAIL SHEEHY*

Whereas the worth of a man may increase
with age in a society ordered by men (so that life
merely begins at forty) that of a woman decreases
with age (so that life ends at thirty).
  ❧ *DALE SPENDER*

It seems the older the men get, the younger their new wives get.
  ❧ *ELIZABETH TAYLOR*

He may be fat, stupid and old, but nonetheless he can condemn
the woman's flabby body and menopause and encounter only
sympathy if he exchanges her for a younger one.
  ❧ *LIV ULLMAN*

Does a man's retirement have to be exile and house arrest?
➤ *June P. Wilson*

Men age better, of course.
➤ *Sally Wilson*
A BEAUTICIAN QUOTED BY NAOMI WOLF

If men's main function were decorative and male
adolescence were seen as the peak of male value, a "distinguished"
middle-aged man would look shockingly flawed.
➤ *Naomi Wolf*

The prime of life, the decades from forty to sixty—
when many men but certainly most women are at the height of
their powers—are cast as men's peak and women's decline
(an especially sharp irony since those years represent
women's sexual peak and men's sexual decline).
➤ *Naomi Wolf*

Men don't age any better physically.
They age better only in terms of social status.
➤ *Naomi Wolf*

If the woman's eyes are his mirror, and the mirror ages,
the gazing man must see that he is aging as well.
➤ *Naomi Wolf*

If I had a nickel for every man who said he didn't
mind being a grandfather but he hated the thought of sleeping
with a grandmother, I'd start a fund for retired grandmothers.
➤ *Betty Jane Wylie*

Older men love the thrill of no underwear because they grew up during a time when women were trussed up in corrective undergarments. Younger men, on the other hand, are bored with bralessness and hygienic cotton shirts. They absolutely adore black lace teddies, push-up bras, and see-through nightgowns.

❧ *BETTY JANE WYLIE*

The memory of most men is an abandoned cemetery where lie, unsung and unhonored, the dead whom they have ceased to cherish. Any lasting grief is reproof to their forgetfulness.

❧ *MARGUERITE YOURCENAR*

SOURCES

Academy Chicago Publishers, Chicago: George Sand, *The Intimate Journal*, ed./tr. Marie Jenney Howe, 1984

American Psychiatric Press, Washington, D.C., London: Malkah T. Notman, and Carol C. Nadelson, *Women and Men: New Perspectives on Gender Differences*, 1991

Arlington House, Inc., New Rochelle, N.Y.: Phyllis Schlafly, *The Power of the Positive Woman*, 1977

Avon Books, New York: Helen Gurley Brown, *Outrageous Opinions*, 1966; *Sex and the Office*, 1983; Kate Millett, *Sexual Politics*, 1971

Ballantine Books, New York: Dr. Joyce Brothers, *What Every Woman Should Know About Men*, 1981; Kim Chernin and Renate Stendhal, *Sex and the Sacred Games* (A Fawcett Columbine Book), 1990; Penelope Franklin, ed., *Private Pages: Diaries of American Women 1830s-1970s*, 1986; Mary Kuczkir, *My Dishtowel Flies at Half-Mast*, 1980

Bantam Books, New York, Toronto, London: Simone de Beauvoir, *The Second Sex*, tr./ed. H.M. Parshley, 1952; Rita Mae Brown, *Starting From Scratch: A Different Kind of Writers' Manual*, 1988, Copyright © by Speakeasy Productions Inc. Used by permission of Bantam Books, a division of Bantam Doubleday Dell Publishing Group; Madonna Kolbenschlag, *Kiss Sleeping Beauty Good-Bye*, 1981, Copyright © Madonna Kolbenschlag, by permission of the author; Merle Shain, *Some Men Are More Perfect Than Others*, 1973

Basic Books, Inc., New York: Mary Field Belenky, Blythe McVicker Clinchy, Nancy Rule Goldberger, and Jill Mattuck Tarule, *Women's Ways of Knowing: The Development of Self, Voice, and Mind*, 1986

Beacon Press, Boston: Mary Daly, *Gyn/Ecology: The Metaethics of Radical Feminism*, Copyright © 1978, 1992 by Mary Daly. Reprinted by permission of Beacon Press; Jean Baker Miller, *Toward a New Psychology of Women*, 1986

Bluestocking Books, Guerneville, Calif.: Laurel Holliday, ed., *Heart Songs: The Intimate Diaries of Young Girls*, 1978

The Bobbs-Merrill Company Inc., Indianapolis, N.Y.: Joan Goulianos, ed., *By a Woman Writ: Literature from Six Centuries By and About Women*, 1973; Maggie Owen Wadelton, *The Book of Maggie Owen*, Copyright © 1941 by The Bobbs-Merrill Company, Inc.

Books, Inc., New York: Mary Field Belenky, Blythe McVicker Clinchy, Nancy Rule Goldberger and Jill Mattuck Tarule, *Women's Ways of Knowing: The Development of Self, Voice, and Mind*, 1986

Jonathan Cape Ltd., London: Nelly Ptaschkina, *The Diary of Nelly Ptaschkina*, ed. Jacques Povolotsky, 1923

Carroll & Graf Publishers, New York: Evelyn Scott, *Escapade: An Autobiography* (first published 1923), 1987, by permission of Carroll & Graf Publishers

Clarke, Irwin & Company, Toronto: Emily Carr, *Hundreds and Thousands: The Journals of Emily Carr*, 1966

Coach House Press, Toronto: Margaret Atwood, *Murder in the Dark*, 1983; *Good Bones*, Copyright © O.W. Toad Ltd. 1992; Libby Scheier, *Second Nature*, 1986, by permission of the author

Collins, London: Margaret Fountaine, *Love Among the Butterflies: The*

Travels and Adventures of a Victorian Lady, ed. W.F. Cater, 1980; Fontana/Collins, London: Joan Wyndham, *Love Lessons, A Wartime Journal*, 1986

Corgi Books, London: Anna Ford, *Men: A Documentary*, 1986

Coventure, London: Beata Bishop, *Below the Belt: An Irreverent Analysis of the Male Ego*, 1977

Crown Publishers, New York: Susan Faludi, *Backlash: The Undeclared War Against American Women*, Copyright © 1991 by Susan Faludi. Reprinted by permission of Crown Publishers, Inc. 1991

David & Charles, Newton Abbot, England: Ellen Weeton, *Miss Weeton: Journal of a Governess* (1807-1825) reprinted as *Miss Weeton's Journal of a Governess*, 1969

Peter Davies, Ltd., London: Jane Rule, *Lesbian Images*, 1976, by permission of the author

Dell Publishing, New York: Nancy Friday, *Men in Love: Men's Sexual Fantasies, the Triumph of Love Over Rage*, 1981; Betty Friedan, *The Feminine Mystique* (reprinted by arrangement with W.W. Norton & Co.), 1963; Phyllis McGinley, *Sixpence in Her Shoe*, 1964; Margaret Mead, *Male and Female: A Study of the Sexes in a Changing World* (Laurel Editions), 1949

Deneau Publishers, Toronto: Elizabeth Smart, *By Grand Central Station I Sat Down and Wept*, 1981; *Necessary Secrets: The Journals of Elizabeth Smart*, 1988

Dodge, New York: Helen Rowland, *Reflections of a Bachelor Girl*, 1909; *The Sayings of Mrs. Solomon*, 1923

Donohue, Henneberry, Chicago: Fanny Fern (pseudonym of Sara Willis Parton) *Fern Leaves from Fanny's Portfolio*, 1853

George H. Doran, New York: Alice Duer Miller, *Are Women People? A Book of Rhymes for Suffrage Times*, 1915

Doubleday, Garden City, N.Y.: Barbara Ehrenreich, *Hearts of Men* (Anchor Press), 1984; Barbara Ehrenreich and Deirdre English, *Re-Making Love: The Feminization of Sex*, 1987; Jean Kerr, *Please Don't Eat the Daisies*, 1957, and *The Snake Has All the Good Lines*, 1960; Anne Szumigalski, *Woman Reading in Bath*, 1974; Kathryn Weibel, *Mirror Mirror: Images of Women Reflected in Popular Culture*, 1977; Joyce Wood, *Are Children Neglecting Their Mothers?*, 1974

Duell, Sloan and Pearce, New York: Phyllis McGinley, *A Pocketful of Wry*, 1940

E.P. Dutton, New York: Andrea Dworkin, *Woman Hating*, Copyright © 1974 by Andrea Dworkin, used by permission of Dutton Signet, a division of Penguin Books USA Inc.; Barbara Pym, *A Very Private Eye: An Autobiography in Diaries and Letters*, ed. Hazel Holt and Hilary Pym, 1984; Gail Sheehy, *Passages: Predictable Crises of Adult Life*, 1974, 1976

Edgepress, Inverness, Calif.: Mary Anne Warren, *The Nature of Woman: An Encyclopaedia and Guide to the Literature*, 1980

Eveleigh Nash, London: Emmeline Pankhurst, *My Own Story*, 1914

Faber & Faber, London: Eva Figes, *Patriarchal Attitudes*, 1970; Liz Lochhead, *The Grimm Sisters* (NEXT Editions), 1981

Fawcett Crest, by arrangement with Harcourt, Brace & World, Inc., New York: Peg Bracken, *The I Hate to Cook Book*, 1966; Appendix to *The I Hate to Cook Book*, 1968; *The I Hate to Housekeep Book*, 1968

T. Fisher, Unwin, London: Charlotte Perkins Gilman, *The Man-Made World or Our Androcentric Culture*, 1922

Golden Heritage Press Inc., New York: Margaret Fuller, *The Wit & Wisdom of Margaret Fuller Ossoli*, compiled and edited by Laurie James, 1988

Goodread Biographies, Saskatoon: Candace Savage, *Our Nell: A Scrapbook Biography of Nellie L. McClung*, 1979

Guernica, Montreal: Maryse Pelletier, *Duo for Obstinate Voices* (a play), 1985, tr. Louise Ringuet, 1990

Harcourt Brace Jovanovich, New York, London: Virginia Woolf, *The Diary of Virginia Woolf, Volume One, 1915-1919*, ed. Anne Olivier Bell, 1977; *The Diary of Virginia Woolf, Volume Two, 1920-1924*, ed. Anne Olivier Bell, assisted by Andrew McNeillie, 1978; *A Room of One's Own* (A Harvest/HBJ Book, San Diego), 1929/1957

Harper/Collins (Triad Grafton Books), New York: Virginia Woolf, *A Writer's Diary*, 1953

Harper Colophon, New York: Louise Bernikow, *Among Women*, 1981; Kim Chernin, *The Obsession: Reflections on the Tyranny of Slenderness*, 1982; Dorothy Dinnerstein, *The Mermaid and the Minotaur*, 1977; Barbara Walker, *The Skeptical Feminist: Discovering the Virgin, Mother, and Crone*, 1987

Harper & Row (Perennial Library), New York: Kim Chernin, *Reinventing Eve: Modern Woman in Search of Herself*, 1988; Susan Griffin, *Rape: The Power of Consciousness* (San Francisco), 1979; Jane Wagner, *The Search for Signs of Intelligent Life in the Universe*, 1987; Barbara G. Walker, *The Crone: Woman of Age, Wisdom, and Power*, 1985

Harvard University Press, Cambridge, Mass.: Carol Gilligan, *In a Different Voice*, Copyright © 1982 by Carol Gilligan, reprinted by permission of the publishers

Hodder & Stoughton (Coronet Books), London: Fay Weldon, *Letters to Alice: On First Reading Jane Austen*, 1984 (Rainbird/Michael Joseph, 1984), Copyright © Fay Weldon, 1984

Henry Holt and Company, New York: Gloria Steinem, *Outrageous Acts and Everyday Rebellions*, Copyright © 1983 by Gloria Steinem. Reprinted by permission of Henry Holt and Company, Inc. Mary Thom, *Letters to Ms., 1972-1987*, 1987; (Praeger Publishers) Elizabeth Friar Williams, *Notes of a Feminist Therapist*, 1976.

Holt, Rinehart & Winston, New York: Alice Koller, *An Unknown Woman: A Journey to Self-Discovery*, 1982

Hounslow Press, Willowdale, Ont.: Henriette Dessaulles, *Hopes and Dreams: The Diary of Henriette Dessaulles, 1874-1881*, tr. Liedewy Hawke, 1986

Hutchinson, London: May Sinclair, *A Journal of Impressions in Belgium 1914-1915*, 1915

Indiana University Press, Bloomington, Ind.: *Women's Autobiography: Essays in Criticism*, ed. Estelle C. Jelinek, 1980, citing Cynthia S. Pomerleau from "The Emergence of Women's Autobiography in England"

Inner City Books, Toronto: Marion Woodman, *The Ravaged Bridegroom: Masculinity in Women*, 1990

Key Porter Books, Toronto: Betty Jane Wylie, *Everywoman's Money Book* (with Lynn MacFarlane), 1984; *Successfully Single*, 1985; *All in the Family*, 1988

Alfred A. Knopf, New York: Nora Ephron, *Crazy Salad: Some Things About*

Women, 1975; Florida Scott-Maxwell, *The Measure of My Days*, 1979, Copyright © 1968 by Florida Scott-Maxwell, reprinted in the U.S.A. by permission of Alfred A. Knopf, Inc. and in Canada by permission of Hilary Henderson; Laurel Thatcher Ulrich, *A MidWife's Tale: The Life of Martha Ballard, Based on her Diary, 1785-1812*, 1990

Lester & Orpen Dennys, Toronto: Jane Rule, *A Hot-Eyed Moderate*, 1985, by permission of the author

Little Brown & Company, Boston: Louisa May Alcott, *The Journals of Louisa May Alcott*, ed. John Myerson and Daniel Shealy, 1989; Gloria Steinem, *Revolution from Within: A Book of Self-Esteem*, 1992

Macfarlane Walter & Ross, Toronto: Marni Jackson, *The Mother Zone: Love, Sex & Laundry in the Modern Family*, 1992, by permission of the author

Macmillan, London: Josephine Butler, *Education and the Employment of Women*, 1868; New York, Toronto: Marie Lénéru, *Journal of Marie Lénéru*, 1923; New York: Margaret Mitchell, *Gone With the Wind*, 1964

McClelland & Stewart (New Canadian Library), Toronto: Anna Brownell Jameson, *Winter Studies and Summer Rambles in Canada*, 1990; Penney Kome, *Somebody Has to Do It: Whose Work is Housework?*, 1982; Emily Murphy, *Janey Canuck in the West*, 1975; Erika Ritter, *Ritter in Residence: A Comic Collection*, 1987

McGraw-Hill, New York, Toronto: Letty Cottin Pogrebin, *Family Politics: Love and Power on an Intimate Frontier*, 1983

Methuen, London: *Plays by Women*, ed. Micheline Wandor (Pam Gems, "Dusa, Fish, Stas & Vi" in vol. 1, 1982; Maureen Duffy, "Rites" in vol. 2, 1983; Liz Lochhead, "Blood and Ice," in vol 4, 1985; Pam Gems, "Queen Christina" in vol. 5, 1986, ed. Mary Remnant)

William Morrow & Co., Inc., New York: Deborah Tannen, *You Just Don't Understand: Women and Men in Conversation*, 1990

Ms. magazine, Copyright © Lang Communications Inc., New York

W.W. Norton & Company, New York: Mary Berenson, *Mary Berenson: A Self-Portrait from Her Diaries and Letters*, ed. Barbara Strachey and Jayne Samuels, 1983; Alice Dunbar-Nelson, *Give Us Each Day: The Diary of Alice Dunbar-Nelson*, ed. Gloria T. Hull, 1984; Margaret Fuller, *Woman in the Nineteenth Century*, 1971; Carolyn G. Heilbrun, *Reinventing Womanhood*, 1979; *Writing a Woman's Life*, 1988; Robin Morgan, *The Demon Lover: On the Sexuality of Terrorism*, 1988

Olympia Press, New York: Valerie Solanis, *Scum Manifesto*, 1968

Open Books, Shepton Mallet, Somerset: R.E. Dobash and R. Dobash, *Violence Against Wives: A Case Against the Patriarchy*, 1980

Oxford University Press, Canada: Margaret Atwood, *The Animals in That Country*, 1968, © Oxford University Press Canada, 1968; *The Journals of Susanna Moodie*, 1970, © Oxford University Press Canada, 1970; *True Stories*, 1981, © Margaret Atwood, 1981; reprinted by permission of Oxford University Press Canada; Mary Boykin Chesnut, *The Private Mary Chesnut: The Unpublished Civil War Diaries*, ed. C. Vann Woodward and Elisabeth Muhlenfeld, 1984; Gerda Lerner, *The Creation of Patriarchy*, 1986; L.M. Montgomery, *The Selected Journals of L.M. Montgomery, Vol 2: 1910-1921*, Mary Rubio and Elizabeth Waterston, co-editors, © University of Guelph, 1987, reprinted by permission of the University of Guelph, Oxford University Press, Canada, and Mary Rubio and Elizabeth Waterston

Paladin (Granada Publishing), London: Germaine Greer, *The Female Eunuch*, 1971 (third printing)

Pandora Press (Unwin Hyman), London: Dale Spender, *Man Made Language*, 1980; Dale Spender, *Women of Ideas, and What Men Have Done to Them*, 1982

Panther Books, Ltd., St. Albans, Hertfordshire: Doris Lessing, *The Golden Notebook*, 1973

Penguin Books, USA Inc.: Regina Barreca, *They Used to Call Me Snow White...But I Drifted: Women's Strategic Use of Humor*, 1991; Carol Cosman, ed., *The Penguin Book of Women Poets*, with Joan Keefe and Kathleen Weaver, 1983; Katherine Mansfield, *The Letters and Journals of Katherine Mansfield*, 1988; Dorothy Parker, "Social Note," Copyright 1928, renewed © 1956 by Dorothy Parker; "The Waltz," Copyright 1933, renewed © 1961 by Dorothy Parker, from *The Portable Dorothy Parker*, Introduction by Brendan Gill. Used by permission of Viking Penguin; Barbara Pym, *Excellent Women*, 1985; Sei Shonagon, *The Pillow Book of Sei Shonagon*, tr./ed. Ivan Morris, 1967; Anne Truitt, *Daybook: The Journal of an Artist*, 1988; Fay Weldon, *Letters to Alice: On First Reading Jane Austen* (Rainbird/Michael Joseph, 1984), Copyright © Fay Weldon, 1984

Playwrights Press, Toronto: Betty Jane Wylie, *A Place on Earth* (a play), 1982; *How to Speak Male* (a play), 1990

Pluto Press, London: Caryl Churchill, *Cloud 9*, 1983

G.P. Putnam's Sons, New York: Alexandra Penney, *Great Sex*, Copyright © 1985 by Alexandra Penney

Quality Paperback Book Club, New York: Christine de Pizan, *The Book of the City of Ladies*, tr. Earl Jeffry Richards, 1992, by arrangement with Persea Books, Inc., Copyright © Book-of-the-Month Club, Inc.

Quill, New York: Susan Connaught Curtin and Patricia O'Connell, *Real Women Send Flowers: A Celebration of Life, Love, and Lust*, 1983

Random House, New York: Etty Hillesum, *An Interrupted Life: The Diaries of Etty Hillesum, 1941-43*, Copyright 1981 De Hann/Uniebock, b.v., English translation copyright 1983 by Jonathan Cape Ltd., published by arrangement with Pantheon Books; Charlotte Perkins Gilman, *Herland: A Lost Feminist Utopian Novel, 1915* (Pantheon Books), 1975; *The Charlotte Perkins Gilman Reader*, ed. Ann J. Lane (Pantheon Books), 1990; Doris Lessing, "Play with a Tiger" in *Plays by and about Women*, ed. Victoria Sullivan and James Hatch (Vintage Books), 1974; Clare Boothe Luce, "The Women," play, copyright 1937, renewed 1965, published in *Plays By and About Women* (Vintage Books), 1974; Robin Morgan, ed., *Sisterhood is Powerful: An Anthology of Writings from the Women's Liberation Movement* (Vintage Books), 1970; Camille Paglia, *Sex, Art, and American Culture*, Copyright © 1992 by Camille Paglia. Reprinted by permission of Vintage Books; Sophia Tolstoy, *The Diaries of Sophia Tolstoy*, tr. Cathy Porter, 1985; Jill Tweedie, *In the Name of Love: Love in Theory and Practice Throughout the Ages* (Pantheon), 1979; Naomi Wolf, *The Beauty Myth*, Copyright © 1991 Naomi Wolf. Reprinted by permission of Random House of Canada Limited

Routledge & Kegan Paul, London: Mary O'Brien, *The Politics of Reproduction*, 1981; Routledge, London & New York: Elspeth Graham, Hilary Hinds, Elaine Hobby and Helen Wilcox, eds., *Her Own Life: Autobiographical Writings by Seventeenth-Century Englishwomen*, 1989

Rutgers University Press, New Brunswick, N.J.: Harriet Blodgett, *Centuries of Female Days: Englishwomen's Private Diaries*, 1988

St. Martin's, New York: Nicole Hollander, *The Whole Enchilada: A Spicy Collection of Sylvia*, 1986

Seal Books: McClelland-Bantam Inc., Toronto: Margaret Atwood, *Cat's Eye*, Copyright © 1988 by O.W. Toad, Ltd.; Stewart-Bantam, J.B. Lippincott Company, New York: Merle Shain, *When Lovers Are Friends*, Copyright © 1973 by Merle Shain

Secker & Warburg, London: Germaine Greer, *Sex and Destiny: The Politics of Human Fertility*, 1984

Simon & Schuster, New York: Susan Brownmiller, *Femininity*, 1984; Phyllis Chesler, *About Men*, 1980; Cynthia Heimel, *Sex Tips for Girls*, 1983; Lois Wyse, *The Six-Figure Woman (and How to Be One)*, 1975

Stein and Day, New York: Reay Tannahill, *Sex in History*, 1980

Frederick A. Stokes Co., New York: Mary MacLane, *I, Mary MacLane: A Diary of Human Days*, 1917

Herbert S. Stone, Chicago: Mary MacLane, *The Story of Mary MacLane, by Herself*, 1902

Talonbooks, Vancouver: Betty Lambert, "Under the Skin" (first published in 1987 by Playwrights Canada), in *Twenty Years at Play*, ed. Jerry Wasserman, 1990; Betty Lambert, "Sqrieux-de-Dieu," 1976

Taplinger Publishing Company, New York: Paula Modersohn-Becker, *Paula Modersohn-Becker: The Letters and Journals*, ed. Gunter Busch and Liselotte von Reinken, ed./tr. Arthur S. Wensinger and Carole Clew Hoey, 1983

Times Change Press, Ojai, Calif.: Emma Goldman, *The Traffic in Women and Other Essays on Feminism*, 1970

University of California Press, Los Angeles: Nancy Chodorow, *The Reproduction of Mothering: Psychoanalysis and the Sociology of Gender*, Copyright © 1978 The Regents of the University of California

The University of Chicago Press, Chicago: Elizabeth K. Helsinger, Robin Lauterbach Sheets and William Veeder, *The Woman Question, Volume I: Defining Voices*, 1989; *The Woman Question, Volume II: Literary Issues*, 1989; Patricia Meyer Spacks, *Gossip*, 1986

University of Illinois Press, Chicago: Janice Delaney, Mary Jane Lupton, and Emily Toth, *The Curse: A Cultural History of Menstruation* (revised edition), 1988

The University of Iowa Press, Iowa City: Judy Nolte Lensink, *"A Secret to be Buried"; The Diary and Life of Emily Hawley Gillespie, 1858-1888*, Copyright © 1989, by permission of the University of Iowa Press

University of Minnesota Press, Minneapolis: Nancy A. Walker, *A Very Serious Thing: Women's Humor and American Culture*, 1988

University of Toronto Press, Toronto: Elizabeth Smith, *A Woman with a Purpose: The Diaries of Elizabeth Smith, 1872-1884*, ed. Veronic Strong-Boag, 1980

Virago Press (Penguin Books), London: Fidelis Morgan, ed., *The Female Wits: Women Playwrights of the Restoration*, 1981; New York: Kay Boyle, *Year Before Last*, 1986

Warner Books, New York: Sonya Friedman, *Men Are Just Desserts*, 1984; Dr. Ruth Westheimer, *Dr. Ruth's Guide for Married Lovers*, 1986

Warner Paperbacks, New York: Francine Klagsbrun, ed., *The First Ms. Reader*, Copyright © 1973 Ms. Magazine Corp.

J.R. Wilkin, London: Mary Astell, *A Serious Proposal to the Ladies for the Advancement of their True and Greatest Interest*, 1701; quoted in *The Meridian Anthology of Early Women Writers*

Wollstonecraft Incorporated, Los Angeles: Victoria Billings, *The Womansbook*, 1975

The Women's Press, London: Tierl Thompson, ed., *Dear Girl*. The extracts from *Dear Girl* edited by Tierl Thompson, first published by The Women's Press Ltd., 1987, 34 Great Sutton Street, London, ECIV ODX, are used by permission of The Women's Press Ltd.

World Publishing, New York: Jessie Bernard, *The Future of Marriage*, 1972

COLLECTIONS

Adams, Abby, ed. *An Uncommon Scold.* New York: Simon & Schuster, 1989

Bartlett's Familiar Quotations, 15th Edition. ed. Emily Morison Beck. Boston: Little, Brown and Company, 1980

Brown, Michele, and Ann O'Connor. *Hammer & Tongues: A Dictionary of Women's Wit and Humour.* London: J.M. Dent & Sons, 1986

Cole, William, and Louis Phillips, eds. *Sex: "The Most Fun You Can Have Without Laughing."* London: Pan Books, 1990

Colombo, John Robert, ed. *Colombo's Canadian Quotations.* Edmonton: Hurtig Publishers, 1974

——— *The Dictionary of Canadian Quotations.* Toronto: Stoddart Publishing Co., 1991

Cooper, Jilly, and Tom Hartman. *Violets and Vinegard: Beyond Bartlett, Quotations By and About Women.* New York: Stein and Day, 1982

Gould, Allan, ed. *The Great Big Book of Canadian Humour.* Toronto: Macmillan, 1992

Guterman, Norbert, ed. *The Anchor Book of French Quotations.* New York: Anchor Books/Doubleday, 1963

Hamilton, Robert M., and Dorothy Shields, eds. *The Dictionary of Canadian Quotations and Phrases.* Toronto: McClelland & Stewart, 1982

Maggio, Rosalie, ed. *The Beacon Book of Quotations by Women.* Boston: Beacon Press, 1992

Mencken, H.L. *A New Dictionary of Quotations: On Historical Principles from Ancient and Modern Sources.* New York: Alfred A Knopf, 1962

Partnow, Elaine, ed. *The Quotable Woman: An Encyclopaedia of Useful Quotations Indexed by Subject and Author, 1800-1975.* Los Angeles: Corwin Books, 1977

———— *The Quotable Woman: An Encyclopaedia of Useful Quotations, Volume Two, 1900-The Present.* Los Angeles: Pinnacle Books, 1980

The Quotable Woman. Philadelphia: Running Press, 1991

Rogers, Katharine M., and William McCarthy, eds. *The Meridian Anthology of Early Women Writers: British Literary Women from Aphra Behn to Maria Edgeworth, 1660-1800.* New York: Meridian/New American Library, 1987

Rowes, Barbara. *The Book of Quotes.* New York: Ballantine Books, 1979

Sternburg, Janet, ed. *The Writer on Her Work.* New York: W. Norton & Company, 1980

Sumrall, Amber Coverdale. *Write to the Heart: Wit & Wisdom of Women Writers.* Freedom, Calif.: The Crossing Press, 1992

Warner, Carolyn, ed. *The Last Word: A Treasury of Women's Quotes.* Englewood Cliffs, N.J.: Prentice Hall, 1992

Warren, Mary Anne. *The Nature of Woman: An Encyclopaedia and Guide to the Literature.* Inverness, Calif.: Edgepress, 1980

Winokur, Jon, ed. *The Portable Curmudgeon.* New York: New American Library, 1987

BIOGRAPHICAL INDEX